THE MOST EXPENSIVE MISTRESS IN JEFFERSON COUNTY

To Maria
Best wishes always
Jim Misko

A Novel
By James A. Misko

Other books by the Author:

Fiction:

For What He Could Become
The Most Expensive Mistress in Jefferson County

Non Fiction:

Creative Financing of Real Estate
How to Finance Any Real Estate Any Place Any Time
How to Finance Any Real Estate Any Place Any Time –
    Strategies That Work

For information regarding special discounts for bulk purchases, please contact Northwest Ventures Press book sales at 907-562-2520.

Designed by:
Endpaper map courtesy of
Back cover endpaper courtesy of

Manufactured in the United States of America

10 9 8 7 6 5 4 3 2 1

Library of Congress Control Number:

ISBN

Misko, James A.   1932 -
     The Most Expensive Mistress in Jefferson County.

Published by:
Northwest Ventures
3820 Lake Otis Parkway, Suite 201
Anchorage, AK 99508
website – www.JimMisko.com
author's email – Jim@JimMisko.com

DEDICATION

Dedicated to the thousands of people who bought my
first novel and proved to me and others that there
are readers who want entertainment, education, and
inspiration in a novel.

Chapter 1

4:09 a.m. June 8, 1998 Monday

The phone rang. He forced one eye open and looked at the clock. It was 0409 hours. He made a mental note to change the clock back to a.m. and p.m. tomorrow. That crazy air force woman was always changing the clocks.

"Hello," he said.

"Hi. You in bed?"

"Yes."

"Asleep?"

"Not now."

"Roger just took off up the river. He wants to be there by six. Your door unlocked?"

"You know it is."

"I'll be over. Bye."

Sue Diggs sure has a sweet voice on the phone. Especially when she wants something. I wonder if I can perform twice in one night? Might be I can.

He lay in bed with his eyes closed listening to the occasional traffic on the road to the lake. In the state of half sleep he recalled his beginnings with Sue at the marina.

"But you're married," she said.

Hawk pulled on his lower cheek. "So are you."

Her smile was infectious. His eyes took in her dark short lean endowed body. When he looked up a smile crept across his face and their eyes had a mutual understanding.

He tipped up his beer. She did the same and within an hour they each had five empties stacked beside them. He had never drunk that many beers and later he recognized it as a purposeful distraction to avoid what was happening between them; a brief blocking and prolonging of the inevitable.

"Let's take a boat ride," he said.

Sue giggled, her eyes coy under the dark eyelashes. "I don't know if I can walk let alone get in a boat." She stood up and he held her arm. He wasn't very stable either.

During the time they spent getting the boat, the marina operator showed some concern as to their sobriety and ability to run it. After they had been shown how to start and operate the motor, Hawk went back and got another six-pack, grinning like a high school kid when he set the frosty beer under the seat.

For the first fifteen minutes they motored close to the bank until they came to a passage between the shore and a small island covered with scrub brush.

Sue pointed to the island. "Let's go over there." Then she stood up, the boat tilted and for a moment she was parallel to the water, her laughing face looked at him before she was enveloped in the water.

Like drawing a pistol, Hawk whipped out his wallet, threw it in the boat and dived in after her. He cupped his arm around her and towed her to shore while she coughed and spit and laughed. While they sat on the shore chuckling, a gentle breeze shoved the boat up on the sand. Hawk secured it and grabbed the beer. When he turned around Sue was half undressed, demurely hanging her wet clothes on a small bush. He stood looking at her, his passion rising.

"Well…" she said. "You gonna let them dry on or off?"

Like teenagers, they held each others' naked body, kissing hard, thrashing around on the hot sand. Hawk tried several times to penetrate her but she was very adept at deflecting that opportunity. She grabbed him with her hand.

"Come on," he pleaded.

She giggled. "Try this," she said and began stroking him with her hand.

That was the first of many meetings. It laid the foundation for both divorces.

What if she never came over again? How would I feel about it? Put the pluses and minus's on a T-sheet and see the result. Plus: she's pretty, sexy, intelligent, fun to be with. Minus: lousy family, argumentative, distrustful, petty, can't handle money worth a damn. Hell—that gives her more minus' then pluses.

He heard the door open and the squeak in the 3rd step coming up to the 2nd floor. He opened one eye and looked down the hallway. Nothing. He heard rustling of clothing and then the streetlight shining through the window fell on her body as she came through the open door. It was a body to behold for a woman who had given birth to three kids. He could feel his loins strengthening and he gave no more thought to whether he could or could not perform again.

At 5:30, or 0530 by the clock he awoke and started to the kitchen. From the door to his bedroom and down the hall to the landing the woman's clothes were scattered. He stepped on her bra with his bare foot and realized it was padded. He hadn't noticed that. Course he never undressed her anymore. She took care of that.

He dumped a damp load of clothes into the dryer then opened the cupboard and took out the Rogaine. Standing in front of a full length mirror on the wall he smeared it on his head with his left hand while the other pulled the refrigerator door open and poured a cup of V8 juice. The light was not that good but he could follow the thinning rows of blond hair as he tilted his head toward the mirror. He noted also the grey bags under his eyes—nonexistent four years ago, a gift from this deal that was now coming to a climax. He took a body builder's pose, flexed and let his eyes drift over each set of muscles; the tightened abs showed a fine line of demarcation from his rib cage, his arms and shoulder muscles tight and traceable to their connecting joints. He was reasonably happy with what the new weight lifting regimen was doing for him. Then he upended a paper cup of vitamins into his mouth and flushed them down with three swallows.

The window framed the backyard, lush with native and exotic flora starting their first bloom of the year; the hot tub was a late addition to the big house that sat on the only hill in Rapid City overlooking the river. It was the only house in town he had lusted for. He had driven by it a hundred times, watched the owners grow old, saw the property deteriorate, planned and hoped how he would acquire it. Now that he owned it, he had halted the deterioration, added some to the landscaping. It was a financial drain the last three years and only his equity, which he kept borrowing against, was keeping him afloat financially.

He smiled. He should have been sitting in a rocking chair mostly blind and barely able to walk with his damaged back. At age fifty he could have spent the rest of his life being looked after by one of his sons in the big house beside the

Sturgis River. But cataract surgery was a wonderful thing—it restored his vision to 20-20 and a neurosurgeon installed titanium discs between his deteriorated backbones.

That he could walk and see now was a blessing he thought about every day. In his life there had not been much time for self-analysis, other than a scratch moment or two before dawn. Born on a poor ranch in the scablands of Eastern Washington, he had worked hard from dawn to dark all his life. All things were laid out as soon as he was old enough to understand tasks in relation to daylight hours. Even before daylight he milked the cow, gathered the eggs, fed the chickens, and ran the milk through the separator. When it was light enough he could do regular farm work, mend fence, chase down stray cattle that had gotten out, cut fire wood, repair equipment and do school work.

There were folks who had more time than money who analyzed people's lives and they had told him more times than he cared to remember, that he was the skip generation. His grandfather—tough as rawhide—had talent and drive. It was what was left of the ranch his grandfather had established, that his father, stepmother, stepbrother, stepsister, and he lived and worked themselves to death on.

The good land was gone. Sold off to pay his fathers gambling debts, personal errors of judgment and flagrant misunderstanding of how the formation of capital and the use of money functioned in the world in general and in one's family life in particular. His father would have at one time been considered a 'coupon clipper'; one who's forebearers had left enough wealth for the family to invest and receive monthly checks. Even through the depression of the late 1930's his family had lived comfortably. He had not known that time; only this time and he had vowed to not just survive, but to prosper like his grandfather.

Every time he pulled an egg from under a clucking hen, stacked a chunk of fire wood, lifted a bucket of milk, or drove a staple into a fence post, he vowed that he would rise above this;

would live in the best house in town; drive the best car; that he would match and then exceed his grandfather.

It was almost dawn on Monday, June 8, 1998. He stood barefoot in the kitchen, looking out at the bubbling spa in the backyard and about to start the 1258th day of work on a $400 million dollar real estate transaction. His name was Hawkins Neilson and upstairs asleep in his bed waiting for the sun to rise was Sue Diggs, the most expensive mistress in Jefferson County.

He lifted the phone and dialed a number from memory. Slim and Reba Collins would be awake by now, having their morning coffee and listening to the stock reports. In the southeast corner of Jefferson County, on a chunk of ground that leaned up against the Coburg Mountains, they farmed some 600 acres and ran cattle over the remaining 3,200 acres that had been homesteaded by Colonel Rhett Collins in 1878.

"Morning, Slim. You ready to trade for that six hundred forty acres today? We gotta close it up this week or Fish and Game is gonna back off the deal—and you know—we're never sure of the Indians."

A slow voice scarred by fifty years of cigarette smoking came over the phone. "Hawk—you didn't even let me finish my morning coffee." He held the phone away from him and coughed.

"Me and the wife been talking it over. We aren't gonna do the deal. That six hundred forty is nothin but rocks and rattlesnakes. That's why the government still owns it and it wasn't in the original homestead. It's just not worth the prime riverfront you're wanting us to trade for it. What I really want is some of that high meadowland up on Buffalo Lake. Get me an acre for acre trade of that and I could get interested."

There he goes again. Hawk dropped his head, his brain in gear for an answer. The signal on the clothes dryer squawked and he walked into the utility room to shut it off.

"Slim—you know and I know that they're not goin' to

bust into that park and cut you out some lakefront. It would make an inholding that they don't have now and it wouldn't straighten out their boundary line or solve their problem."

"Well…" Slim hesitated. "We're just not in the mood to make it easy for them. The sons-a-bitches have been makin it hard for me for twenty-five years."

Hawk took a deep breath. "Slim—don't say no just yet. Hang in there with me on this and I'll get something you like better but I need time—ok?"

"I got time till I die then you'll have to deal with the wife and kids and they'll be a damn sight tougher than I am."

"I'll get something—soon." He pulled the hot clothes out of the dryer and laid them across the washer, a chair, a small table.

"That's what you've been saying for more'n three years now Hawk. Don't those people have any sense of when to get things done?"

"Some do. But I'm fighting a whole bureaucracy you know."

"Yeah I know. Fight the good fight. I'll be hayin' down on the low land this week so don't bother callin' me until Friday. And drop down here next time you're in the area, we'll hoist a few and talk man talk."

Hawk heard another cough and then the phone rattled in the cradle. "Dammit, dammit, dammit!" He slammed his fist on the counter.

Hawk showered, dressed, took a quick glance at Sue lying in the bed with the sheet tucked under her arm. How could she sleep when this deal was unraveling every day? He left his shoes off until he got to the garage, grabbed his keys and let the car ease down the driveway until it was well away from the house before he let the clutch out and started it on compression.

7:15 a.m. Monday, June 8, 1998

His usual booth was waiting for him at Ella's Café, a

relic of the gold rush logging days complete with a screen door with holes in it and a spring that pulled the thing shut against the frame. The smell of diesel truck fumes emanating from the street and bacon frying inside vied for olfactory dominance as he slid in on the red plastic seat broken down by the weight of big men for twenty years. He opened the Spokesman Review, checked the track scores then threw the paper on the table. The waitress slipped a cup of coffee to him as she passed and said "Usual?" Hawk nodded.

Going over the conversation with Slim he tried to think of anything he had left out, anything that would make a reasonable swap for Slim other than the high meadowland he wanted.

Hell—he wouldn't give up riverfront for that inholding either, but BLM insisted it was a fair trade, their appraisers had said so and they were sticking to it. Sitting in Boise in an office supplied by the government, driving a government car, with a government credit card—what did they know of a rancher's daily bargain with the land?

"Morning Hawk," a familiar voice burst through his thoughts.

Hawk turned to see Carroll Swenson, president of Wesco Bank, standing beside the booth. "Hello Carroll."

"Wish you'd drop by the bank as soon as you're done here."

Hawk looked up at him with a question in his eyes.

"Why don't you come to the back door around 9:00 o'clock? I'd like to talk to you as soon as possible."

The waitress brought Hawk's breakfast and slid it across the table with one hand while she poured him more coffee with the other. "Morning Carroll," she said. "You got any financing for boats?"

"What kind of boats?"

"River boats. Those things cost several thousand now days."

"Sure. You buyin' one for Carl when he retires to keep him out of your hair?"

"Just five days a week," she laughed.

"Sure. We'll finance it if you give us all your tips for payment."

"That'd take a hundred years."

"Not from what I see you pick up." Carroll's eyes narrowed. "Do you report those to the IRS?"

"Just yours. You're the only one who keeps track of what you leave."

She moved on.

"You having breakfast?" Hawk said.

Carroll picked up the discarded paper, folded it and put it under his arm. "I did."

"Why don't you just sit down and tell me what you want here and now?"

Carroll glanced around. "I'd rather do it in my office."

Hawk turned the eggs over and covered them with black pepper. "I'll be by."

Carroll wrinkled his nose, "I couldn't eat like that," he said, and turned to leave.

Hawk finished eating in seven minutes while his mind drifted over the possibilities of what the banker wanted to talk about.

He and Carroll went back a long ways. Being a year younger than Hawk, Carroll had always had a bit of trouble playing with the big boys but by high school he had fleshed out enough to handle the end spot on the football team, shot well enough to be a basketball forward and was fast enough to run a fair 880. They had lost touch when Hawk had gone to agricultural college and Carroll traipsed off to the University of Oregon, took business courses and after graduation started working for a small bank in Bend, Oregon.

But as strange as this world is, when Hawk wanted to start a second bank in town to rival the one that thought they had preemptive rights to every dollar that flowed through Rapid City, he went looking for a bank president who could pull in local deposits because he could talk their language and would have their full faith and trust. He found Carroll, who had progressed up the corporate ladder to senior vice president, whose wife was longing to get back to Rapid City, and whose kids would be a reasonable asset to the high school sports program. He made him an offer he couldn't refuse.

Title—President, and all the glory that goes with it, a five year contract with extensions if it worked well, a salary that would put him in the upper two percent of the population in Jefferson County, and an option on enough bank stock to allow him to retire when he was sixty-five if it went well. Hawk never discussed or even thought about it not going well. Carroll thought about it all the time.

Hawk stopped at the cashier on the way out, where over the intervening years of his life, Jessie Hahn had gone from a comely eighteen-year-old cheerleader to a comfortable, chubby, pleasant, know-everybody-and-their-business cashier.

"Morning Hawk. Cash or credit?" she said.

"Put it on my account will you Jessie?"

"Sure." She pulled out the credit book, opened a page and ran her finger down the column. Her finger stopped and she looked up. "Ella's gonna want some payment on it pretty soon. It's getting up there."

"Yeah—I know."

She took a pen and wrote the numbers.

He pushed the screen door open and stepped out on the sidewalk. His gaze fell on a logging truck stopped at the red light, loaded with twenty-five to thirty small trees, their tops no more than six inches in diameter. The air was colored with diesel fumes.

Pecker poles. Was it true that all the high quality trees were cut out of Jefferson County? When he was in high school the trucks often had only two or three logs for a load.

7:45 a.m. Monday, June 8, 1998

Hawk opened the door to Jefferson County Realty and smiled at the mounted game heads on the wall, the morning

light reflecting from their glass eyes. He tilted his head and
ran his eyes over each mount, recalling the hunt, the stalk, the
shot. Thirty years of his life were represented on the wall and
he wanted to never forget the days in the field. He relived the
hunts to keep them fresh in his memory, to not forget the sights
and sounds and smells of standing in the backcountry alone,
shivering in the cold dawn, listening to the bugle of a bull elk,
watching the smoke of his breath in the frozen air or turning
to hear rock tumble from sheep climbing out of a deep canyon.
He had pitted his two legs against their four, his powder and
lead against their sense of hearing and smell and had won often
enough to have a fine head collection. And he had not been
a wastrel with the meat or hides. The meat was eaten, if not
by him and his family, by others who needed it, and the hides
tanned and given to Indians on the reservation who manufactured items from them to sell.

"Mornin' beasts," he said.

The mounted heads were mute.

He walked to his desk and flicked on the voice mail.

"First message: Mr. Neilsen, this is David Bires calling.
I'm a field representative for the Internal Revenue Service in the
Boise office. We have some concerns regarding your reported
sale of a house in your 1996 returns and just as a housekeeping
item, we'd like to audit your books for the last three years. This
is just a superficial audit to try and get a feeling for your income
and expenses. We'd like to be there Wednesday if that's a good
time for you. You can reach me at…"

Hawk shook his head. He listened to the other messages
and then cleared them. He stood up, closed his eyes, stretched
his head back over his shoulders until he felt his back pop. He
usually got two or three pops as the discs slid back and then he
could stand and think straight.

At 8:00 a.m. Wev and Ruthann came in with sixteen
ounce Lattes in hand.

"Morning brother," Wev said.

Hawk looked at him. "What's this brother stuff?"

"Ruthann said a lot of people didn't know we were brothers and I should take to calling you that more often."

Hawk glanced at Ruthann opening up her desk for the day. She had once been pretty but the addition of forty pounds hadn't done her body any good although it did smooth out her face.

"Well—being a step brother doesn't mean the same thing and I don't see any reason for you to go around town calling me brother. Sounds like some sort of black man's game, and Ruthann shouldn't—."

Ruthann burst in. "When's the deal gonna close Hawk?"

Damn her! She knows the closing date as well as anyone.

"This week. Got to. Too much hanging on it," he shot back.

Hawk slammed the door behind him and jaywalked across the street, down the alley and knocked on the back door of the bank. He saw Carroll Swenson turn, smile, get up from his leather chair and start for the door.

A woodpecker was working on the mulberry tree behind the Sandstone Bar and the sound mingled with the smells from the garbage cans pulled out in the alley. This alley hadn't changed its smell in twenty years. It took Hawk right back to grade school when he'd walked through it on his way home.

There was the little pocket behind the garbage cans between the Bar and Shakey's Pizza Parlor where he had hid on initiation night while the seniors were searching out the freshmen. That was the first time in his life he could remember being frightened. Tales of being left naked fifteen miles out in the country and being forced to walk back to town or having to smoke an entire cigarette inhaling every puff until you puked your dinner up, pervaded the freshman class, and while no one actually knew anybody who had had to do these things, it was assumed that someone in their class would.

"Thanks for coming in Hawk. Just need a few minutes."

Carroll led into the conference room, closed the door slowly and quietly with both hands.

"Looks like it's gonna be a nice day…" Carroll started, then trailed off.

"Nice enough," Hawk said.

Carroll had his hands on the tabletop with the fingers interlaced. He looked at them in silence for a moment before looking up. Hawk had seen that same look a hundred times in history class when the teacher asked him a question he couldn't answer.

"Hawk—you need to do something for me on your line of credit. The board meeting is coming up Thursday night and they're gonna insist on some action on it." He took a quick breath and continued. "You haven't made a payment on it for over four months and from what I hear around town your credit at the store and cafe are about to be closed. When's this deal gonna close?"

"Carroll—I need time."

"Dammit Hawk, I've loosened every screw, every binder that's available to me but they won't let me keep ignoring this loan. It is a sizeable amount for our bank you know?"

"Look—Carroll—I worked my ass off getting this bank in here. Got depositor's—big ones to switch banks and help open this place. And I got you out of that lousy bank in Bend to run it. Now I need some help. Time is all I need. When this deal closes my fee alone will double the capital of the bank."

"That much?" Carroll watched Hawk nodding. "How much?"

"It will double your capital."

Carroll looked out the window. "You mean we'd have close to fifty million?"

Hawk nodded again.

Carroll took a deep breath, bent his head back and looked at the ceiling. His lips were pursed and the tips of his fingers had turned white.

"Ok. I'll tell them we need to extend for another—what—ninety days?

"That's plenty."

"You're sure you can pay the full $120,000 by then?"

They both nodded.

Chapter 2

Hawk jerked the door open. Everybody in the office looked up. He walked over to Ruthann's desk. "How much money do we have in the transaction account?" She smiled. "I don't know for sure." "Find out and give me an answer." "It'll take me some time, Hawk." "Get it before lunch." He marched back into his glass office and slammed the door. In a minute he was on the phone. He couldn't believe his own bank was pushing him. RuthAnn pushing him, Slim crawfishing on the land trade. Bureau of Land Management, Idaho fish and Game, Nez Perce tribe, Forest Service, and 160 other land owners all poised to sign the largest land exchange in the history of Idaho and everyone was shoving on him to solve little dinky problems that would all be solved this week. Providing the deal closed.

Stoddard Greening looked up from his computer. "What the hell is that all about?"

Ruthann shook her head. "I don't know. He's just like that lately."

"The kids?"

"Stoddard—I don't know. He doesn't confide in me."

"Hell—everybody knows about them."

"Yes they do don't they!" She stood up, straightened her skirt and sauntered to the bathroom.

She couldn't recall the exact moment she had decided to become abrasive. Whether it was because of her marriage, the utter failure of their children to do what they asked of them, her husband's inability to provide a decent living and his intransigence in dealing with the few investment properties they had, or from Hawk's entire dominance of their business lives of late and by projection, their personal lives as well. But for sure, her thinking had changed dramatically when she was voted Treasurer of the corporation, and she experienced economic power first hand. Bank officers treated her with deference, invited her into their private offices, sent her baskets of fruit and chocolates on holidays, and rolled out the red carpet when she requested personal loans for a new car, to finance a hot tub in the backyard, or fund the college tuition for her son. Eventually she had decided that holding the purse strings and controlling up to a million dollars in front-end money coming in from investors in this deal gave her a tinglely feeling. One she liked.

Ruthann could hardly say $400 Million even in her mind. It was absurd, insane, ludicrous, a masturbation of the ego. She and her husband's share of the fee would be close to three million. A lifetime of dividends. Freedom. Exultation.

She didn't know what to do to speed it up and she wasn't exactly sure how it got to where it was but she was a part of it and she clung to that dream twenty-four hours a day.

In the hot tub last night, she and Wev had toasted the deal with a 1984 San Sebastian Merlot and when the bottle was gone, he had convinced her to turn the tub lights off, take off her suit, and make love with him on the fiberglass seat in the hundred and two degree water.

Stoddard walked over to Wev's desk. "You got any idea?"

Wev shook his head. "While you were in Boise he got worse."

"Anyone talk to him about it?"

"Who's gonna say anything? I'm his step-brother—that doesn't cut any ice with him."

"Well he's the backbone of this whole transaction. If he goes off his nut we'll never get this thing done."

Wev shook his head. "I agree,"

Stoddard shoved his bottom lip over his top one. He froze that way for a minute then stretched. "Goin for coffee."

Wev watched him strut across the street.

That's one way to avoid it. A cup of coffee and a cinnamon roll—take the sour taste out of your mouth.

He pushed back his chair and headed to the coffee shop.

Hawk put his feet on the desk and leaned back in the chair, the phone cradled against his chin and shoulder. For the last two years he had been selling property after property—most of it to Royal Cunningham. When he needed money for the transaction and the funding well had run dry he knew he could always sell some of his real estate for enough to carry him through to the next crisis. He rationalized it as an investment process. He had bought the properties—generally taken as commissions on long ago transactions—and held on thinking of them as retirement vehicles for his old age. He was now gambling these equities as his bet in the highest stake game he had ever been in.

How many cotton-picking times would he be broke before he was at last wealthy?

He knew Royal Cunningham's code and he let it ring ten times until a voice answered.

"This is Royal Cunningham." There was a distinct calmness to the voice.

"Royal—this is Hawk."

"Is this business or social?"

"Dammed if I know. It's getting so I can't tell the difference anymore."

"Well—I'll help you out. Business is where I screw you and social is where you screw Edith."

"Cripes Royal—we've been divorced five years."

"I know, but you can't miss her looks at you when you're in a group."

That's true, he mused. Her eyes followed him from across the room, over a piano, across the restaurant. She would come back to him if he called her, but he couldn't live that way anymore. There was love and passion and then there was a smothering, caustic, eating away of his most inner desires. He had opted out of the marriage.

"For crying out loud that part of my life is behind me," Hawk said.

"Ok."

"I guess it's business," Hawk testified. "I want you to buy the apartments from me."

"Why?"

"I need some working capital." Hawk felt wetness in his armpits.

"You have any equity in that firetrap?"

He's starting again—downgrading my property before he steals it. The first three properties he had sold Cunningham when he was an up-and-comer had been on easy terms because

Cunningham didn't have much money but he did have good credit. Hawk needed the small amount of money he got from the down payment and it was easy to sell the contract because of the buyer's good credit so with a small discount he could get all cash. Now, Royal paid cash for everything and he dealt hard paying rock bottom prices but delivering all cash—sometimes that afternoon.

"Look—you've high graded all my good stuff and now's the time for you to finish the job. I figure an equity of around $125,000."

"How much do you owe?"

"I don't know—around $350,000."

"Well—drop off your income and expense statement. I don't like to own stuff in that part of town but I'll take a look at it. If we make a deal how soon do you need the money?"

"Yesterday."

"Mmmnnn."

Hawk opened his door. "Where's RuthAnn?"

George Arbuckle was the only one in the office. He turned toward Hawk and shook his head, implying he didn't know. "Hawk, come here a minute."

George had a map spread on the top of his desk.

"This is Kootnai County," George said. He put his finger on the map. "The land the Indians want to throw into the deal is back up here. I don't know what good that land is gonna do for the Forest Service to convince them to make the trade."

"Can they even get in to it?"

"Well, they might if BLM would let the Forest Service and Fish and Game cross over the old logging road from Elim to Kootnai. The trouble is that the chief and his counsel figure part of the government _is_ the government so they're all the same and they can make a deal when they want to, but the Indians can't. How's Slim comin along with his thinking on the land?"

"I talked to him this morning. He wants some Buffalo Lake frontage."

George starred at Hawk. "Judas Priest—the forest service will never go along with that."

"Well there's gotta be a way. We've come too far now to let him stop this thing and there's nobody else we can put into Slim's position. We need his land to make the thing work so Fish and Game can get control of the river banks."

George sat back in his chair. "All the time I've been working on this trade I thought there'd come a time when we couldn't move. Too many pieces, too many people, too many things to go wrong and here we've put almost three years into it and I don't know how many dollars and now this."

"We've had "this" before George. We always get by "this". Relax and set up a meeting with the Indians after we talk to BLM and the Forest Service."

"What about Slim?"

"I'll handle Slim."

"I know you've been saying that but he hasn't moved one iota since we first started talking to him. I don't think he's gonna."

"That's not your job George." He jabbed a finger in George's chest. "Set up the meeting!"

George threw up his hands. "Ok. But it's gonna be a short one. They don't want to talk unless we've got agreement with BLM and the Forest Service."

"George—you tell those briefcase Indians we want a meeting!"

As long as they had known each other, George had been heavy, slow, and careful with his thoughts and speech. He didn't talk to be heard or hear himself. He talked when he had thought something out and was prepared to do something about it. It might take several days longer than anyone else would have taken, but almost always, what he came up with was thorough, the negatives well delineated, and the outcome predictable. He kept a container of Costco almonds on the corner of his desk and everyone knew when they heard the lid unscrewing that George was heading into a mental coon hunt and they would have to listen to him crunching almonds while he pondered.

RuthAnn slipped into her chair and opened her computer. Hawk walked over and stood behind her. Her desk was immaculate, dusted, every thing in its place. Even her children's photos framed in old barn wood were in line by age.

"Don't do that Hawk. It makes me nervous."

"Why do you allow the records to get so far behind?"

RuthAnn squirmed more firmly into her chair, straightened her back and looked into the computer screen. "I have a lot of work to do. You notice I don't have any help and these figures change so often with you and Stoddard writing checks on the account all the time."

Hawk's voice lowered and he leaned his head close to her. "I need that money figure now RuthAnn and I want the accounts brought current instead of being ninety days behind. I can't tell anything about how long the funds will last."

"That's a lot of work."

"Well—get to it then. The bank board is meeting on Thursday night and I want to know how much is there. I may need to pay down the credit line."

"They'll go along with you. They always do."

"That's not the point! Doesn't anyone else understand that?" Hawk's face reddened.

She fidgeted in her seat while her fingernails clacked on the keyboard. Hawk couldn't make sense of anything that came up on the screen and he sensed she was not going to produce the document while he stood there. He turned in time to see Wev and Stoddard laughing as they came back across the street.

Hawk walked back to his office and closed the door. He thought for a minute then dialed the IRS office in Boise. While he waited to get through the automated answering system he wondered if he had met David Bires, the IRS Field Agent who had called.

Who might know him and put in a good word for me?

Bires answered the phone. He swallowed as he spoke with a voice that was old, edgy, and tobacco scarred. Reminded Hawk of a college professor he hadn't liked.

"Mr. Bires, this is Hawkins Neilson."

"Yes, Mr. Neilson." He coughed. "Thank you for returning the call. I'm going to be up in your area later this week and I'd like to sit down with you in regards to your 1996 tax returns. Could you make yourself available say on Friday at 10 o'clock?"

"I'd generally be available for that but I'm in the middle of a very important transaction right now that needs to close by Friday. I have no time available until July. Can you work that out?"

"Oh, I don't think so." There was a low hum of voices behind him.

"Just what is it about the return that concerns you?"

"We may have more than one, but the glaring one at this moment is the sale of the house." He took his time to continue. "You claimed it as a residence but it appears," he paused, "to have been a rental and should have been reported as capital gain." Hawk heard him sit up in his chair. "Do you recall that entry?"

"Mr. Bires, I don't do my tax returns and I don't remember. Can it wait until we meet in July?"

"We're a little short handed in this office and the statute of limitations is about to run out on this return. However, if you'd be willing to sign an extension we could postpone the visit until July."

"And what does the extension do?"

"It extends the statute of limitations for a year. Just to give us time to evaluate your return and your answers to our questions. It's just a formality."

Hawk bit the skin on the side of his thumb.

"Mr. Neilson?"

"Yeah—I'm here. I don't like the sound of that Mr. Bires."

"Well—then we really need to meet with you this week. Or you could come down here if meeting you in your office won't work for you."

Hawk drummed his fingers on the desk. "Mr. Bires, I can't do it this week, here or there, and I'm not gonna sign an extension. We'll just have to work out a different time."

"I figured you'd say that so I'm sending an extension to you by FedEx at this minute. You'll have it before 11:00 a.m. tomorrow. I would seriously advise you to execute it to avoid the Service making assumptions about this transaction that could cause you fines and penalties."

"I understand. I'll look at it. What day did you say you'd be up here?"

"I didn't, but it could be Wednesday. If you can find time then it would help the case."

Case? Judas Priest they're calling it a case already.

"Call me when you're in town and we'll see."

"Very good Mr. Neilson. But think seriously about the extension."

Hawk slammed the phone down, crossed his arms and stared at the ceiling. Then picked it up and dialed.

"Law offices."

"Hi, Betty. This is Hawk. Thaddeus in?"

"Oh hi, Mr. Neilson. Yes he is—just a minute."

Hawk could see Wev and Stoddard working at their desks. George was on the phone, his almond eating hand momentarily suspended.

He'd better be talking turkey to the Indians.

"Hawk—to what do I owe the pleasure of your early morning call before my coffee has sufficiently cooled to render it drinkable and thus allow me to participate in the animated conversation that is sure to follow?"

"You know enough about IRS law to help me on an extension or not?"

Thaddeus coughed. "IRS—IRS, oh yes, the Infernal Revenue Suckers."

"The very ones."

"What's up?"

"They want me to sign an extension on my 1996 tax returns for a year. Should I do it?"

Hawk could almost hear him thinking. "Depends. What have they got on you?"

"I don't know. Something about the way I reported income on a house sale."

"I'll look it up if you want."

"How much will that cost me?"

"Typical. A hundred and fifty an hour for research."

"I thought you were educated in law school. I shouldn't have to pay for your learning something you should already know."

"How the hell do you think I make a living?"

"You rob orphans and widows."

"I gave that up for Lent."

"Ok. Get me an answer before tomorrow morning. They want an answer."

"My coffee's cool now. Have a pleasant morning, Hawk."

"Same to you."

9:02 a.m. Monday, June 8, 1998

Hawk stretched then slumped in his chair. His stomach rumbled and he thought about coffee and a roll, then hit his stomach with the flat of his hand and felt the slight paunch that he had noticed developing over the last four years.

Not working out enough. This deal is gonna make me fat, ill tempered, and rich. Hell—when I'm rich I can cure the other things.

He moved his hand around on his belly liking the feel

of it but his abdominal six-pack was no longer there. He'd get back to serious workouts now that his back was finally healing. The Dall sheep's head stared down from the wall, the glass eyes bestowing a calming effect on his built up tension. Step by step he went back over the five shots he had taken to kill the sheep and then its slide down the scree launching itself halfway into an ice cave on the river. Big sheep were hard to find and harder to hunt and he had the biggest sheep head in Jefferson County. He smiled.

Jason Neilson knocked on the door and opened it, displaying a partial grin on his face. Hawk motioned him in. He was taller than his father, very clean and athletic looking.

"Hi, Dad," Jason said.

"Morning, son. What brings you to town?"

Jason cocked his head and let his eyes wander over the trophies on the wall. "Wondering about the deal. Where it is and when it's gonna close…" Jason let the sentence hang, eyes down, his demeanor resembling a beta wolf. If he could have felt good about getting on his knees and licking Hawk's boots, he would have done it. He hated coming in but his choices had run out and he didn't want to be at home when the inevitable came out.

"Friday," Hawk spit out.

"You sure?"

Hawk nodded.

"Can I count on that?"

"Hell no! Who can count on anything in this world." The vehemence of his reply hung in the closed room.

Jason looked out the window, his fingers drumming on the arm of the chair. "You got time for a cup of coffee, Dad?"

Hawk made a mental note of what lay before him and decided there was enough time to have coffee with his oldest son.

"Sure. Let's go." He flung an arm over his son's shoulder and they walked out of the office side by side, two carbon copies of Great Grandfather Neilson whose photo hung over the door of Hawk's office.

At the café Hawk spun a counter stool around. Jason touched his arm.

"Could we take a table, Dad?"

"Maria—would you bring two coffees over to the table please?"

"Your arm busted?" she said.

"No—but I'd like to tip you once."

"Yeah—tip me upside down and take all the money outta my pockets."

"That too."

At a table in the corner, the furthest away from the cash register, Jason pulled out a chair facing the counter, which left Hawk a chair looking at the wall.

"What's your brother doin'?" Hawk opened.

Jason shook his head. "You know Jonathan. Big O Tires jacked his car up when he had it parked on the street and took off the wheels and tires he hadn't paid for. They put on the smallest, ugliest, worn out set of wheels you ever saw."

"You serious?"

Jason nodded. "I don't know what he's livin' on. He's got to have something coming in."

"Yeah—well…." Hawk looked at the high school football calendar on the wall, an annual fund raising event. The café owners were good supporters. He saw where his real estate company's ad was—not in a very good location.

"When you gonna marry that girl you're living with and give me some grandchildren. I need to try my hand at this again since I didn't do so well with you guys."

Jason looked at the tabletop between his folded hands while Maria delivered the coffee. She slopped some when she moved the cup over to Jason and Hawk dobbed a napkin on it.

"Dad—Eva and I broke up last night. I wanted to know if I could move home?"

Move home? Wife and kids gone and I'm gonna start providing a rooming house for them to come back?

"Hell no. I've got my own life to live. Don't need my grown son hanging around my place. You've got money—get an apartment for awhile until this deal closes, then with your share you can get a good house."

Jason pursed his lips. "You remember our deal for me to make the payments on your credit card? I'm ninety days behind. The collection agency left a message on my cell phone giving me until Friday to come up with the back payments."

Hawk, blank faced, slumped in his chair. "Jason—that was our deal. I paid off your debt—you took over my credit card payments."

"I know Dad. But I couldn't handle the payments."

"Why didn't you let me know before you got ninety days delinquent?"

"I thought I could pick them up soon—somewhere along the way—some other deal maybe." Jason looked down at his intertwined fingers.

"Yeah—well—we all think that way don't we?"

Jason nodded.

Hawk looked at the top of Jason's head thinking back to the beautiful baby he had been and how happy he and Edith had been with their first son. So lively, so sharp, so dedicated to what they wanted to teach him. He grew so strong and so fast. Where did those twenty years go? Now he was thirty and broke. Why did I encourage him to go into this business? He could have done anything else; made a reasonable living; enjoyed other people. Now he's bound into this deal and he's in the same crap pot I'm in.

"What happened to the money you had from the last deal?"

"Gone Dad. It's just gone."

"What about the house and car?"

"I mortgaged the house. Guess Carroll didn't mention it to you huh?"

Hawk shook his head.

Jason looked down at his hands. "I'm behind on that too."

Hawk snorted. "Like father like son."

Jason nodded.

Hawk had his entire net worth into the transaction. This deal would make him. It would clear every debt he had and give him a sizeable nest egg, one that would allow him to play for real. Hunting trips to Africa and Scotland and Australia. A company airplane, the house paid off. He'd own his car instead of leasing it. Until now his play had been a side activity. But he had obligations. He was the father. He just had to find a way.

"Well I'll talk to Carroll if you want. They've got a board meeting Thursday and I'm trying to see what we can do to whittle down the line of credit by then. I'll see if there is anything in the pot that we can apply to these problems."

"Thanks Dad."

Hawk shook his head. He threw two dollars on the table and saw Maria looking sideways at the tip. "You make that coffee with river water again? Tasted a bit like you took it from below Edsen Creek."

"If it was below Edsen Creek you wouldn't be walking out of here. We'd be calling 911."

"Call them anyway. I'm not sure I can make it back to my office."

"We've got a guy who walks people back to their offices for a fee."

"I'm sure you do Maria. I'm sure you do."

"You heading by Royal's office?" Hawk asked.

Jason nodded.

"Take these income reports over to him will you?"

"You selling him something else?"

"What the hell do you expect? Everything needs money

around here. We don't have it and Royal does, so I sell him something. Now get out of here."

When Jason left the room Hawk looked at the sheep again. The outside sunlight had moved off the glass eyes and momentarily made ridges of shadows on the horns.

"You had it easy ole boy. Food, water, safety. That's all you cared about. Oh, a little sex once a year but then you just hung out with the boys and napped in the sunlight and kept your eyes out for wolves. If there is reincarnation, I'm coming back as a ram."

9:30 a.m. Monday, June 8, 1998

George Arbuckle knocked on Hawk's door and then let himself in. His shirt was part way out of his pants and bloused over his belt so it made him look fatter than he was. However, he had not fallen into the problem a lot of big, slow, careful men had that of leaving part of their last meal on the front of each day's shirt.

George followed Hawk's gaze. "You'd still rather be a ram?"

"You damn rights."

George laughed. "Well, the Indians are willing to meet but they want Cruit Johnson there and they want it before Wednesday."

"Is Cruit back in town?"

"For right now he is. They let him out last Friday."

"Judas H. Priest," Hawk said. "Now we gotta contend with that crazy."

George massaged his gums with his tongue while Hawk thought.

"Ok," he finally said. "Get a meeting room at the hotel and set it up for Tuesday night, seven o'clock."

"They'll want a drink by then," George said.

"Oh right. How about dinner then—say five o'clock."

"They'll expect you to provide dinner."

"For how many?"

"Probably five plus Cruit. You and me and Stoddard. That's nine."

"Ok. See if you can put it on the company credit card and get back to me on their approval. Tell them no drinking until after the meeting."

Chapter 3

12:01 p.m. June 8, 1998 Monday

Hawk answered the phone. He was the only person in the office.

"Hawk?" Thaddeus started, "I thought I would get to leave a message since it's after twelve o'clock and all you type A people are out to lunch at noon sharp. Anyway, the jist of the IRS argument for an extension is…" Thaddeus coughed, "that if you don't sign it they hit you with all their suspicions, and then—Spanish law in play—they get to watch you squirm around and try and prove your innocence. Did they give you forty-eight hours notice on the extension?"

Hawk thought back. "I think so Thaddeus."

"Well—they're obligated to give you that. You just need to decide whether you want to take the time now or later to resolve their inquiry."

"I sure don't have…"

"Hawk—they gonna find anything else if they look deep?"

"How the hell do I know?" Hawk sneezed.

"God bless you. What does Corki know about it?" Thaddeus could hear him wiping his nose with a handkerchief, and the change in his voice that his sneezes always caused.

"She just keeps the books," Hawk said. "Dee does the tax returns. I'll ask her."

"I see I've run your bill up another Twelve dollars and twenty-five cents with this phone call. You can buy lunch and I'll forgo billing you for it."

"Meet me at Ella's in five minutes—I want to make a call."

Ella's Café was a leftover from the effort by the town council to remake Main Street. It still had the big glass windows on both sides of the inset door, pasted with signs advertising a garage sale, the football schedule for the year, pictures of lost pets, and a battered OPEN sign that could be reversed when Ella closed the place at midnight to read CLOSED to anyone unfamiliar with the hours of operation. It was faced with horizontal pine siding with peeling paint between the glass and the top of the false front. The sign spelling out Ella's Café was sun faded but still readable. The day started before dawn there for a lot of the townspeople and the Rotary Club and the Chamber of Commerce met there at different days of the week. A new restaurant with nicer booths, better lighting, and higher prices had moved in a year ago but the loggers, ranchers, mill hands and old timers didn't leave. They loved the brown sausage gravy spilled over the buttermilk biscuits and the chicken fried steaks that hung over the side of the plate.

Hawk slid into the booth across from Thaddeus Burton who started speaking without taking his eyes off the menu.

"They haven't changed the menu in this place since Jesus was a child."

"Good afternoon Thaddeus. I am happy to see that your usual demeanor is in place and all is right with the world," Hawk said.

"I'm not sure they have enough decent food to take care of my Twelve dollar and twenty-five cent bill. Can we go someplace else?"

"They credit me here," Hawk said.

Thaddeus drained his water glass, then set it down on the table with a sense of finality. "I want to give the food something to sit on."

Hawk ignored him. "Thaddeus—you remember Cruit Johnson?"

"The Indian that wanted to sell the town site back to the city council? The one who threw beer bottles through the chamber windows? The one who brought a pickup load of straw to town soaked in diesel fuel and set it on fire outside city hall? The one who ran for 1,800 yards his senior year and married the home coming queen? No—I don't remember him."

"The Tribe is insisting he be present at our meeting Tuesday."

"Why?"

"I thought you might know."

Thaddeus sat back and let his eyes drift over the booths out the window and into the street. "You know," he started. "There was some talk that he had taken law courses while he was in the big house."

"Do you think he would remember them?"

"He isn't that far gone Hawk. He's still a relatively young man."

"Yeah—but he's been rode hard and put up wet."

Thaddeus made a scowl. "I would be leery of him. He

could be more dangerous than you expect and partly because he could be so unpredictable since…"

"He was always unpredictable," Hawk put in.

"…since," Thaddeus continued, looking down his nose at Hawk for the interruption, "if my memory is correct, they let him out on good behavior. You mix good behavior with law courses and you could face a formidable personage."

"That combination would be a first."

"I don't know why I work with you when you disparage the profession that is the backbone of my livelihood."

"It's the widows and orphans thing that keeps me coming back. I figure if you are robbing them you're passing along the savings to me. Please order counselor and don't let it go above Twelve Dollars and twenty-five cents."

Thaddeus smiled. "How much is the whistling marmot and mongoose stew?"

1:30 a.m. June 8, 1998, Monday

"Good afternoon. Swenson Miles CPA," a sweet voice intoned.

"Hi Corki."

"Hi Hawk," her voice melted in one heartbeat.

"How's your day going?"

"It would be absolutely fantastic if I knew when I'd see you again."

Hawk paused. "The IRS wants to come have a look see at my books. Do you remember a house deal I did back in '95?"

"Noooo. But I'll bet we can find it."

"Can you bring the books and copies of the tax returns and come over Wednesday afternoon after work?"

"Sure. Want me to bring some dinner?"

"If you want. And while you're there show me how to change the clocks back to regular time."

"I thought you were going to learn military time?"

"Corki—I don't have the time to mess with that now. I just need to know what time it is without thinking about it, ok?"

"Pizza ok?" she piped in.

"Fine."

"Mushrooms and sausage?"

"Corki—anything."

"Me in a blanket?"

"That would do. I'll hold you to that."

"I wish you would," she said.

Hawk set the phone down and smiled.

How long had this been going on now? Three years maybe? She came to town with a boyfriend both working for H&R Block at tax time. When she split up with him he left, she stayed. She knew bookkeeping and Hawk was looking around for another way to handle his accounting chores. Having Ruthann continue handling it was becoming a burden on her and an unwanted sharing of personal stuff by Hawk. They met when she worked at the bank then she moved to the CPA firm. She did his books on the side, in the evenings, at his home. One thing led to another and pretty soon it was dinner, books, bed— and not always in that order.

2:00 p.m. Monday, June 8, 1998

"Where you going Hawk?" Stoddard Greening asked.

"Royal's office."

"You selling him something else?"

"What difference does it make?" Hawk said.

Stoddard shook his head. "Doesn't make any difference, but we're awful close to some big money and I'd of thought you'd keep hold of what you've got left."

Hawk stood three inches taller than Stoddard and was a handshake away. "Then you put in the money?"

"Hawk—easy—I don't have any money."

"Then why worry about where I get enough to close this

deal. We're gonna have a $500 dinner bill tomorrow night, my kid's late on paying my credit card, and payroll is coming up a week from now. Do you ever think about that? Does anybody think about that besides me? I don't think so."

Stoddard frowned, frustrated. "You're blowing up a lot lately." He took a step backwards. "I understand."

"No—I don't think you do. If this deal doesn't close; if the ranchers say to hell with the trade and the Indians don't budge, our time limit is gone and we've just thrown $1.2 million down the toilet on environmental reports, drainage reports, fish studies, biological reports, cultural reports, and a thousand nights in motels eating crappy food. And at that point we're dead broke!"

"I know that Hawk." Stoddard's face was creased, the wrinkles extending from ear to ear above his eyes.

"I hear you guys say it but I don't see you bringing in any money." Hawk took a deep breath and whooshed the air out between his clenched teeth.

Stoddard backed up and crossed his arms over his chest. For a minute he stared at Hawk then turned and walked to his desk. He spun the chair around to look out the side window, his back to Hawk.

Hawk looked at Ruthann. She looked him straight in the eye, her fingers resting on the keyboard.

"Have you got that figure yet?" He said.

She shook her head. The half smile on her face mocked him.

Why me? Why today? Does every competent person have an ass assisting them?

"By God!" he bellowed and it happened in an instant.

He intended to leave and moved toward the door, the sound of his steps pounding through the small office. His thumb pushed down the lever. He threw the door open, his breathing coming deeper and faster and a wave passed through him that caused him to blink. And then, before he could judge the act, he jerked on the door. He pulled and wrestled and twisted trying to yank it off its hinges. His foot lashed out and smashed through the center panel. It made a hollow sound, the wood splintering, glass shattering as the top screws pulled out and the whole mess burst across the sidewalk. For Hawk it all happened in silence. Then the sounds drifted in and he stood witnessing the astonished stares of people who had come out on the sidewalk.

Wev was standing with his hands on his hips in the empty doorway. "What do you think you're doing?"

"I'm not carrying the dead wood in this office anymore. I'm outta here!" Hawk said. He stormed away. Before he realized Royal's office was the other direction, he had gone a block.

How the hell am I going to survive this? I can't keep breaking up my team and my office.

"Come in Hawk. Sit down and take a load off your feet."

The chair that Royal sat in was high enough to let him look down on whoever sat in the chair across the desk from him. The walls were upholstered and a soft light coming from twelve sconces at strategic points around the room provided a gentle atmosphere where problems could be addressed in comfort and leisure. It bespoke of surplus cash; enough to pay your bills, invest some, and save some. The smell of leather dressing came from the supple chairs and couch in front of the desk. If you had to sign something, Royal handed you a gold Cross pen that he lifted from its marble base and you reached over and signed it on the desk pad that was trimmed in the same soft champagne colored leather. Hawk took a deep breath and started to relax.

"I've been looking at your reports…"

Hawk crossed one leg over the other. He tried to control his breathing, squeezed his left arm with the right hand while he waited for Royal to continue. But he merely shuffled papers for a moment, then put them in a neat pile, anchored his elbows on the desk and made a steeple with his fingers.

"When can we take a look at the units?" he said.

Hawk swallowed. "I don't want to disturb the tenants until we've got a deal."

"Well—you know I don't buy a pig in a poke. I want to see the goods inside and out…"

"And you will get to do that very thing. But first I want a deal that we agree on and if we can do that, then we'll squire you through it floor by floor, door by door."

Royal lifted his chin off his peaked fingers and stared out the window. "I like to buy at a cap rate that allows for the renovation I know it will need. From your figures I think $395,000 is a very good price." He turned his eyes to look at Hawk.

Hawk held his tongue.

I knew it was going to be like this. Where is my edge? How much do I absolutely need to make it through to the closing…if it closes? Verify the money first.

"You can write me a check today?" Hawk asked.

Royal nodded.

"$450,000."

Royal shook his head.

"Look—we can run this game back and forth for an hour. What would make you happy?" Hawk said.

"$400,000."

"My God Royal—that's about half the replacement cost on those units."

"Perhaps—but they need renovation and the rents are not going to escalate that much. I told you I don't like to buy in that part of town and that's one of the reasons, the rents are just not commensurate with the rest of town. Laid off loggers, mill hands, truckers who beat up their wives every Friday night and every one of them shows you a pistol if you go to collect late rent."

Hawk ignored the comment. "Make it $425,000 and I'll show you the units."

Royal pointed a finger at Hawk. "I'll go the $425,000

but it must be contingent upon my approval of the property. I've just seen it from the street."

　　　"Fair enough."

　　　That's only $75,000 for my equity—half of what it's worth—did I figure right? Is that enough to get this thing done?

　　　A shiver moved up his spine to the back of his head. He took a deep breath. There was always an excitement when he made a quick deal. It came from not knowing if he was right, if he had left money on the table…a thousand things.

　　　"When do you want to see them?"

　　　"Friday morning ok?" Royal said.

　　　Hawk twisted in his chair. "Royal—I need the check today. Friday's too late."

　　　"I've got my day planned. I can't do it today. Let's see…"

　　　"You look this afternoon and cement the deal today…or no deal."

　　　Royal hesitated. Hawk could read his mind. He had known him since high school and while the silence ate up the time he framed the questions going through Royal's mind. He needs to think about it. He needs time. What will his Mom think—she's against any more local real estate anyway. But at $425,000 it's a good deal …a $100,000 profit in a year.

　　　Royal took a deep breath. "Ok. I'll meet you there at five o'clock."

　　　"Needs to be at three. I want the check in the bank by five."

　　　Royal bit his lip. "I don't know why I let you have your way all the time."

　　　"Because I'm giving you some easy money. Probably $100,000 in a year."

　　　"I was thinking maybe—just maybe--$25,000," Royal replied.

　　　Outside and halfway down the block, Hawk let out a

holler. Jean Brite, who had been standing in the entryway of her used book store stuck her head out.

"Was that you, Mr. Neilson?" she said, arms crossed over her chest. "Are you ok?"

"I'm fine, Ms. Brite. Just a bit of good news to celebrate."

She smiled. "That good to hear. Everyone should have some good news."

"Indeed they should. Indeed they should. Have a pleasant day."

She nodded and retreated to her entryway to wonder what the good news was. She would never ask but if she took her coffee at Ella's in the morning Jessie would know. Jessie always knew everything.

4:25 p.m. Monday, June 8, 1998

Carroll was sitting at his desk when Hawk came through the door and slipped into the chair. He slid the check for $75,000 across the desk and Carroll studied it, then smiled.

"Is it good?" Carroll asked.

"You ought to know. It's written on your bank," Hawk said.

"You paying off the line?"

"No...not all of it. Use that to convince the Board to extend the line and put that in my transaction account. On second thought...put it in my personal account."

"I'd say so. Your transaction account has plenty in it."

Hawk's jaw dropped. "Really?"

Carroll lifted the phone and dialed accounting. While he waited he cleaned his fingernails with a bent paper clip. Hawk put it in the back of his mind to buy him a nail clipper with the file and cleaner on it at his next birthday. Maybe a gold plated one in a little leather holder. That wouldn't be too fancy for Carroll. With the thought that he had access to more money than he figured earlier, he was feeling expansive and relaxed.

"Thank you," Carroll hung up the phone. "One hundred twenty thousand," he said.

Hawks eyes narrowed. He clenched his teeth and rejected the first thoughts that came to his mind. RuthAnn must have known this. Didn't tell me. Kept it a secret. Was it possible she didn't know it herself? Could she really be so far behind that she didn't actually know? She and Wev have a big stake in this deal—why would she sabotage me like this?

"Just a minute—I'll get you a deposit receipt," Carroll said and walked boldly to the teller's cage where he waited for the receipt.

It would be quite a feather in his cap with this young teller, handing her a check this large to process for him while his important client sat at his desk. He let his eyes drift over her exposed cleavage as she did her work and noted the panty line running across her thigh. I need to ask her out for a drink. Maybe the day after the Board meeting…Friday…that would be an opener.

She handed him the receipt and her eyes and smile told him he would not be disappointed if he ever got up the nerve to ask. Yes…Friday would be a good day.

4:49 p.m. Monday, June 8, 1998

When Hawk saw the maintenance men working on the front door he slipped through the alley and came in the back. Stoddard and George were holding down the fort. Hawk looked at Ruthann's desk. It was clean, the computer covered, the drawers locked. He tried all the drawers. Every one locked. He kicked the chair across the room.

"Where the hell did she go?" he bellowed.

"Easy, Hawk," George said. "It's almost quitting time."

"Almost…but not quite and I need those figures."

Stoddard picked up a sheet of paper. "She left this."

Hawk snatched it out of his hand and read it.

"Hawk. I don't know what's gotten into you lately but you can't just order me around like a servant. I am an integral part of this office and this transaction and it means as much to Wev and me as it does to you. I can't do ninety days of accounting in half a day and do the other things around here too. I'll work on it and get it for you as soon as I can." It wasn't signed.

Hawk slammed the letter down. "What else does she do? Make coffee, answer the phone?"

"Come on, Hawk. She closes deals too," Stoddard pleaded.

"We haven't had a closing in a year and a half and we're not gonna have any more if this thing falls apart!"

Stoddard and George looked at each other.

It was interesting how they each chose the same stance when they didn't know what they wanted to say in a discussion. Or maybe an argument. Cross their arms and install a blank face. Maybe it's me. I chose them—made them part of this team—maybe those are the people I'm comfortable with—the ducks that swim together on the pond. Not the eagles. He shook his head. Self-examination bored him. He debated about calling RuthAnn at home. Some payments must have been made on old deals to have that much money in the account. She isn't telling me about it. Why?

4:52 p.m. Monday, June 8, 1998

RuthAnn sat at the New Account desk in Wells Fargo Bank.

"What name do you want on the checks?" the vice president asked.

"Liberty Funding," she said.

"Is that a corporation?"

"No. An assumed business name."

He slid two cards across the table to her. "Get these signed and we'll have the checks by next Monday and in the meantime, here are six temporary checks."

She signed one card and gave it back to him. "Here's my signature card, I'll get the other one signed and bring it back."

"Ok—that's fine—but you'll be the only one who can write checks on this account until we get the other card."

"Yes—I understand."

"Thank you, Mrs. Neilson for the large deposit and for the trust of your business."

She offered him her hand. "Thank you for staying late to handle this for me. Goodbye."

"Goodbye, Mrs. Neilson." He watched her leave the bank then clapped his hands. "We got it!" The two remaining employees looked up. "We got it—right out of Wesco Bank into ours."

There weren't many $100,000+ accounts in the valley and since he had come to town he could only name a half dozen such accounts. Most had fled to the new bank when it opened, promising no-cost checking, high interest rates on deposits, and a congenial staff that thought the customer was king. Their stock had been eagerly sought and most of the people in town had a few shares to brag about. Now he had just nailed one of those accounts down. He frowned. What had he done to get it? What aspect of his management could he look to for credit? He'd have to ponder that while he had a double Manhattan at Swenson's Swizzler.

"Good night girls. Lock it tight—we're a little richer tonight than usual."

RuthAnn sat in her car, the late sounds of the town running through the windows. Shouted greetings across the parking lot, a loud car radio, a screen door slamming on the funeral home. Had she thought of everything? Would this move prevent Hawk from using the funds to pay his personal line of credit—not save it for the transaction costs? They all had so much riding on this.

She alone knew the account balance. She gave Hawk the figures he used. She alone could sign on the new account until at least Monday. It looked good. The money would be there under her protective care.

RuthAnn started her car and began the slow uphill drive home. A smile crept across her face and then she started to sing, something she hadn't done for a long time. The words came back and even through the rust of years of not singing she was not unhappy with the sounds that filled the car. She opened the window to let the world know her rhapsody.

Chapter 4

5:30 p.m. Monday, June 8, 1998

Hawk poured two ounces of Lagavulin Scotch whiskey in a glass and sat in a lounge chair on the patio overlooking the Sturgis River. The last rays of the sun shone in his eyes before it dropped behind the hills. He raised the glass in a salute, "To absent friends."

The whiskey burned the back of his throat then warmed the path to his stomach. The relaxing came seconds after and he took in a big breath and watched the sun flatten out, turn deep red and disappear. He set the glass down and folded his arms across his stomach.

The usual sounds drifted up from the river. Fishermen, the muffled sound of boat oars, occasionally a word or two. He swatted a mosquito. Often he would go to the river and cast for steelhead; his waders belted snuggly, the opaque line flashing in a figure eight until the fly settled on the water and drifted downstream. The idea passed through his mind but he sipped the whiskey and passed on fishing in preference to the hundredth recounting of the benefits each party would get in this real estate transaction.

He lumped all the private owners together, some 130 of them. They were each getting more land or better land than they were giving up. All had agreed except for Slim who was holding out for high country rangeland in exchange for his river frontage. The Forest Service was getting land with good access and good tree growth potential. BLM, at last, was going to straighten out its boundaries in the scab country and could then offer some of the land to that new mining company in Spokane. The Indians would end up with land abutting the reservation zoned for commercial use.

He threw back another swallow. The Indians and Slim were the last two holdouts. The Indians were almost there until today and now the intrusion of Cruit Johnson threw an unknown into the equation. What would Cruit demand? And why Cruit? Why not the lawyers they had used before?

When this deal was done he was through. It was a clean thought. He had pumped everything he owned into this transaction, selling lots, apartment houses, a motel and his Dad's farm. He had the house, a leased car, and the clothes on his back. The lack of ownership had cleaned up a dusty corner of his life. Other associations, partnerships, corporations, limited partnerships, joint ventures had all been eaten up by the greedy money needs of this transaction. Money for experts to determine the mineral resources, the biological inhabitants, including the botanical growth and the whole, inclusive, stunning, all pervasive, in depth cultural report that took in everything early man had done on that land since the earth cooled.

Why is it that government gets into everything that man does? My grandfather made most of his own rules. Did they ruin it for us? Did the strong ones who made this country, who built the fences and cut the timber and knocked out the grizzly bears and wolves, ruin it for their children and grandchildren? When a man works all of his adult life to just live he becomes like an animal taking nourishment and shelter where he finds it seven days a week. There is no storing up of wealth if you miss the brass ring, just survival. Survival isn't good enough for me. I don't know what the Indians are up to but by God, they aren't going to derail this deal. This one needs to go together. I need that good pull, that high I get when another piece comes in, when I can hold them together for a common goal. And one that will make me the biggest payday of my ever-loving life.

He sipped his whiskey. Who would know how Cruit was thinking and more than that—would tell me?

He pulled out his cell phone and dialed a little used number.

"Hello Hawk," Edith said. He remembered her voice from all of his youth.

"How'd you know it was me?"

"Caller ID. Newest thing in Boise. What's it like on the river tonight?"

"Quiet. A few mosquitoes but not bad."

"To what do I owe the pleasure of this call?" his ex-wife asked.

"Have you seen Cruit Johnson lately?"

"Why do you ask?" she said.

"I need to know what he's thinking. I've got a meeting with the Nez Perce tomorrow night and the Indians want him there. I've got no cotton-pickin' idea why, except he's strong on rights and land claims."

"Exactly."

"Exactly what?" Hawk said.

"You remember when we were married…and we took that trip to Mexico…and we met that lawyer and his wife from

Boise name of Banovich? He worked in native land claims and we had some good conversations down there about the Mexican land rights."

"Yes." Hawk cradled the phone on his shoulder and sipped the whiskey.

"Banovich's offices are down the hall from ours and I saw Cruit coming and going out of there last week. Didn't think anything of it until now. He sure looks good now; all cleaned up, haircut…buff."

"You always had your eye on him…"

It was silent on the other end of the line.

Hawk let it go.

"Suppose Banovich would tell you what they're up to—the Indians?"

"I doubt it. Can you think of any attorney who'd spill info on a client?"

"Yeah…several, but they're all disbarred."

"My point exactly."

It was silent for a few seconds.

"Hawk…you coming down this way? I'd buy lunch."

"Won't be for awhile Edith. I've gotta close this deal by Friday and I still need to satisfy the Nez Perce and Slim."

"Slim always had an eye for me. Tell him I'll sleep with him if it goes to escrow."

"That's all I need. Use my ex-wife as a bribe in a federal transaction. That could be jail time."

"You've done everything else?"

"That's not fair Edith."

"I know it. But it wasn't fair when you kicked me out either."

"We've been over that a hundred times. Let it lay."

He could hear her breathing and pictured her picking a fingernail with her thumbnail like she always did when she talked on the phone.

"If this doesn't go—doesn't close—will it upset your payments to me?" She asked.

"Hell yes. I'll be broke."

"Oh…you'll figure out a way. You always do."

Hawk clinched his jaw. "Yeah. That's what Ruthann said today. Little biddy. She is hiding money on me for some reason but it was too late today to get it straightened out. To-morrow is going to be some day. "Well—thanks. Talk to you later."

"Hawk? Don't always call when you need something… ok?"

"Yeah." He pressed the end button.

He tipped the glass back and stood up. How could thirty years have gone by so fast? Both son's grown…gone—still causing problems—Edith divorced and living with a guy in Boise—and him on the edge of bankruptcy; half a bottle of Scotch and a cord of firewood between where he stood this minute and financial ruin. He shook his head and took a deep breath. The night always made him feel pessimistic. Then he smiled. Edith had taught him to close his eyes and listen to music that moved him—at full volume. It brought him into full con-sciousness and everything he did for a short time after that was golden. Hell—he'd just deposited $75,000 which was more than most men made in a year; the bank would extend his credit line; and somehow the Indians and Slim would have a 'come to realize' and this deal was headed for closure. The darkness covered the river and the trees and was reaching for the top of the mountains as he strode up the lawn leaving the outdoors to the night bugs.

6:30 p.m. Monday, June 8, 1998

Hawk opened a can of chili and dumped it into a pan. There was an opened can of Pepsi in the refrigerator and he tasted it. It was flat as a cold pancake. He poured it out. He pulled out a new can and popped the lid with one hand while he put the newspaper and eating utensils on the bare table with the other. He heard the back door open and close.

"Get away from there—you don't know anything about making food," Sue Diggs said.

"I know if the burner gets hot the food gets hot," Hawk said.

Sue looked at the chili standing upright in the pan.

"That's not food. That should only be stored in case of earthquake or war. That's the kind of stuff you give away when the postal service is collecting food for hungry people."

"I am a hungry people."

Sue set an oven dish on the stove. "You gonna make me a drink?"

"What're we having?"

"Some of that turkey you blasted this spring. It's got enough lead in it to turn the meat gray—what'd you shoot it with?"

"Shotgun." He handed her a glass.

"Put it on the table will you? I'm serving this stuff, dressing and all. I had to take it home to cook it. You don't have a big enough pan here, besides that I didn't want to clean your oven when it popped all over."

"What're we gonna do with the chili?"

"Put it on the patio to cool."

"Some stray dog'll eat it."

"Good. We can sit here and watch him die."

7:30 p.m. Monday, June 8, 1998

"Does that feel good?" Sue said.

"You bet it does."

"Roll over Hawk and I'll do the other side."

He felt the muscles relax and he closed his eyes. Her warm oiled hands moved over his body with practiced skill, touching each place long enough to remove the tension but not enough to excite him.

"What's the matter? Don't think I'm up for it again?" Hawk said.

"Not today honey."

"Humph."

"Just relax and clear your head for tomorrow."

He was really a lucky guy. Forget the close-to-bankruptcy stuff. When you could feel this good, your stomach full and a woman like Sue making every muscle in your body relax and smile—well, what else did a man need?

Was it the money or was it the pure joy of putting the thing together? For twenty-five years he had closed deal after deal, generally short term stuff. Built his holdings until he had a goodly number of properties that should have taken care of him as they became free of debt and started putting cash flow into his pockets. That should have been about now. But he got started trying to solve everybody's problems. The Bureau of Land Management, the Fish and Game, ranchers, Indian tribes. Everybody wanted something they didn't have and he was the guy that could straighten it out and get paid doing it.

She was rubbing his legs now and he closed his eyes and concentrated on her fingers moving the large thigh muscle back and forth, her hands sliding smoothly over the oiled surface.

"That's doing it," he said. "Where'd you learn how to do this?"

Sue chuckled. "I read it in a book."

"Yeah? Why?"

"The title was Relaxation Massage Therapy. My guess was that you'd need a lot of this before this deal closed and if it was going to get this intimate, I wanted to be the one to do it."

"Hmmm. You ever get jealous?"

There was a moment of silence. "No."

"You sure?" Hawk said.

"Well—I could I suppose."

"What would it take?"

"Why? You want to find out? Why don't you just lie there and let this work for you. You need it something fierce—

your muscles are all tied up. Just relax and think good thoughts. Think about closing this thing. Three years is too long and everyone's wondering if it will really happen."

"It'll happen," Hawk mumbled.

"Ssshhh—we've heard that before. Just rest. Relax."

Sue Diggs. A quiet pretty local girl who married her high school sweetheart right after graduation and proceeded to shell out three children in five years. She stayed true and loyal to her husband until he started working so far away he was only home on weekends and she ended up at her tenth high school reunion alone. There, despite her feeble efforts at remaining aloof she ran into Chad Rainey who regaled her with the stories of his financial success in contracting, how he had always admired her, and convinced her that he and his wife were parted. They agreed to meet again and this time he suggested they view the valley from his airplane. A couple of flights later and they were flying to small towns along the river, landing and visiting a motel. For three years she had a standing date at the airport every Wednesday at 2:00 p.m. until Chad misjudged a downdraft coming over Lolo Pass and drove his plane into the granite face of Erin Peak. She was morose for six months, only going out of the house to do the shopping. Her kids noticed it a little; her husband not at all.

Then she started working in real estate. It came naturally to her and she had the charm and openness to get people to do what worked for them. What worked for them usually worked for her as well. She made a good deal of money in the early years, built up some equities and some debts, and then, as her children matured and her husband became more distant, she spent the money and the equities and was wondering what to do next when she met Hawk at the realtors meeting at the marina. He needed some help in his real estate work and she needed some steady income. Seemed to work for both of them.

When he awoke she was gone, the dishes were done, food in the refrigerator and a blanket over his body. He got off the massage table and went to bed. He opened Trump's THE ART OF THE DEAL to page 125 and began for the hundredth time to ponder what he could put into this deal that would allow it to close on Friday. The light was on and his finger was jammed in page 129 when he woke up and went to the bathroom.

10:30 p.m. Monday, June 8, 1998

Hawk dialed the phone.

"Veterans Club," a voice answered.

"Is Cruit Johnson around?" Hawk asked.

"Yeah, he's here. Cruit…phone."

There was a muffled exchange that Hawk couldn't make out, then the rasping sound of a rough palm sliding away from the mouthpiece.

"Hello…"

"Hi Cruit. Hawk Neilson here."

The phone line went silent.

Hawk looked at the phone then dialed again.

A voice answered, "Veterans Club."

"Hi. I was just talking to Cruit Johnson and the line went dead. Could I speak to him again please?"

"He just left. Sorry."

"Yeah? Ok."

Now what do you suppose that was all about?

Hawk turned on the TV and channel surfed until he found a golf game being played in Palm Springs. The calmness of the green turf game was a contrast to what was going through his mind. It wasn't until he heard the mourning dove's calling that he fell asleep with a plan.

Chapter 5

After setting fire to a load of diesel soaked straw during a city council meeting to bring attention to his disagreement with their proposed ordinance banning Indians from establishments that sold alcohol, Cruit Johnson further lost the city father's endorsement by crashing his pickup truck through the front doors of the city hall to bring attention to the fire outside. That stunt netted him five years in prison and a fine of $3,000.

He adapted to prison life well enough but found most of the prisoner's dependant on others so he quickly rose to a position of leadership. During the first six months there was talk, but no action, and Cruit thought action was the defining difference between somebody who lived his life and somebody who merely spent his time on earth. He enrolled in the prison law courses.

On the sixth month plus two days, Chuck Colson's Prison Ministries came to the 'crowbar hotel' and Cruit joined up. He gave up tobacco, alcohol, and drugs and bought into the entire story of Jesus Christ. The first letter he wrote to his wife pleaded for her to come back, that he was a changed man and would prove it when he got out. What he wanted was a chance.

Walking the streets of Rapid City after his release, he walked into a Nazarene Church and stood quietly looking around. He heard a door open. Soon he felt a presence behind him.

"Could I help you?" the presence said.

"I'm looking for a church to join," Cruit said.

"What brings you here?"

"The door was open."

"I see." The presence extended his hand. "I'm the pastor. Ray Huber."

"Cruit Johnson."

"Well, Mr. Johnson. Why don't you come to our service tomorrow morning and get a good feel for our congregation. We meet at 11:00 o'clock."

"I think I'll do that. Thank you."

"Who was that?" the secretary asked when Pastor Huber returned to the office.

"A man by the name of Cruit Johnson, inquiring of our service."

She stiffened. "You probably haven't heard of him, have you?"

He shook his head.

"Just as well," she said.

He smiled and continued work on his sermon.

After the service, Cruit tracked down one of the elders who had been introduced from the podium.

"The service was well and good, but when are we going to do the stuff?" Cruit said.

"Stuff?" the elder asked.

"Heal the sick—raise the dead—"

"Oh—we believe it—we don't do it here—but we believe it."

Cruit rocked back on his heels. "I gave up drugs for this!"

At Gold's Gym the trainer looked at Cruit's chiseled arms and chest, the clean definition of his calves.

"You haven't been idle," she said.

"Not much to do in there."

"You want a spotter on that heavy weight?"

"I think I can handle it."

He took a deep breath, let part of it out, and pressed the weight off his chest and above him locking his elbows at the top of the move, then let it slowly back down until it rested on the bench brackets.

"Wow. Pretty impressive. That's 300 pounds isn't it?" she said.

He sat up and nodded. "I try it every week to make sure I can still do it." He looked around. "Not many people in here today."

"No. Not on Sunday. Day of rest you know. You going to work out much longer?"

"I'll be about an hour. Is that ok?"

"Ok by me. I'll be in the office if you need anything?"

"Such as…?"

She smiled and winked. "You know—anything."

Cruit snorted. He hadn't looked at another woman since he married Sonja. And in state prison and there wasn't any looking to be had.

"Tell Sonja hello from me," she said.

He looked at her with surprise. "Yeah—I'll do that."

At supper time the house was full of family. The white people called it an extended family, but to the Nez Perce it was THE family. From grandfather to grandson, three generations worked, lived, and hunted out of the house sitting on a small plot of ground within the reservation, locally known as the rez. When they needed anything other than the vegetables they grew in the garden or the deer and elk they killed twelve months a year on the rez, they drove into Rapid City

Tonight's special was venison stew with last year's potatoes and some fresh vegetables from the garden. The chickens were especially proud of their production and since the refrigerator was overflowing with eggs, grandma had cracked and cooked eight eggs in the stew juice. No one had ever known her to do that before but it was tasty.

"When you going to try and see her?" Grandpa asked.

Cruit shook his head. "Haven't decided yet."

His father looked at him. "She living alone?"

"I don't know."

"If you want her back you'd better make a good plan. She's probably made another life without you by now."

"I've only been gone a few years."

"You can have a baby in one year," his father said.

Cruit stopped chewing. He looked at the rest of the family who had frozen in time then put down his fork and excused himself.

Cruit took the phone into the bedroom and closed the door.

"Hello."

"Hi Mrs. Rasmussen. This is Cruit. Is Sonja there?"

"Well hello, Cruit. We'd heard you were back. Is everything ok?"

"What do you mean by 'ok'?"

She stammered. "I mean—are you well, are you looking for work, are you going to stay in Rapid City…." She took a breath and stopped.

"All of the above. Is Sonja there?"

"No—no she isn't."

"Will she be there sooner or later?"

"I'd better have you speak to her father. Orville…."

Cruit could hear conversation but it was difficult even with his good hearing to tell what was said. He heard only one statement—'you tell him that'.

"Hello, Cruit," Orville Rasmussen said.

"Hello Mr. Rasmussen."

"Look, Cruit—while you've been—gone, other things have happened and it wouldn't do anybody any good to stir up old memories now. Surely you can see that can't you?"

"Mr. Rasmussen. Is Sonja living there or not?"

"Now see here, Cruit, you can't just come waltzing back into town and expect everything to be the same as it was when you left. There are things…"

"I'm not interested in things, Mr. Rasmussen. I'm interested in knowing if my wife is living in your house or not."

"Do you have a house…"

"That isn't the point is it? Is she there or not?"

He could hear Mr. Rasmussen's labored breathing. Carefully he replaced the phone in the cradle and walked out the back door.

"Hey, Cruit. Heard you were back in town. Join us for a beer."

"Hello, Randy. I'd take a coke."

"A coke? What have you got against a good cold Bud?"

Cruit pointed to his head. "I got talked out of that."

He got a coke and sat in the booth with old high school friends. The Rapid City Veterans Club smelled like all the bars in the West; stale beer, cigarette and cigar smoke, the wet pungent smell of chewing tobacco rising from the spittoons and musky bodies. Several lights were out and those that weren't were dusty and dull. It was a place like home. Once you got used to it there was a comforting feel to it, a warmth that enveloped you when you left the gravel parking lot and stepped in the door.

"Any of you guys know where Sonja is living?" Cruit asked.

They all looked at each other.

"Cat got your tongues?"

"Naw, Cruit. Just none of us wants to be the one to tell you," Jensen said.

Cruit tilted the coke and finished it in one long draught. Then he set it down in the middle of the table and looked at his former teammates.

"We've been friends long enough that you know you can tell me anything. What I've been through has been tough. What could be so tough about what I'm asking you to do?"

He looked at them individually. "Jensen—you opened holes for me in the toughest defensive lines in the state. Can this be as tough?"

"Yeah, Cruit—it is."

Cruit spread his hands out wide. "Where is she?"

Randy looked him in the eyes. "Promise you won't drive your truck through the front door if I tell you?"

They all chuckled. Cruit smiled and nodded.

"She's living with Jonathan Neilsen in a trailer park up around the bend."

"Hawk Neilsen's kid?" Cruit said.

Randy nodded.

"What's he doing for a living?"

"Nobody knows for sure. He made a big bunch of money buying and selling timber land a year or so ago but I heard he filed bankruptcy last month. We see him around town from time to time. Sonja too."

"She pregnant?" Cruit asked.

"Not that I know of."

Cruit laid the empty bottle on its side on the table and spun it, using his index finger to spin it faster and faster. Then in a flash and with expert timing he slammed his hand down on it stopping it instantly.

"Where do I find this trailer court?" he said, his voice as calm as he could make it.

"You just go up river about a mile and a half and it's on the right hand side. Riverside Park—you can't miss it."

The phone rang and the bar tender answered it. Then he put his hand over the mouthpiece: "Cruit—phone."

"Hello."

"Hi, Cruit. Hawk Neilson here."

Cruit placed the phone in the cradle, waved to his friends and walked out the side door into the parking lot.

Chapter 6

6:02 a.m. Tuesday, June 9, 1998

Hawk woke up with a stiff neck. The massage had relaxed him so much he slept in the same position all night and now he could not turn his head to the left. In the shower he let the hot water run on it until it dissolved the massage oil and loosened his neck so he could turn 15 degrees.

The first thought, after getting some flexibility into his neck, was why the Indians were balking so close to the end. Somehow he had to find out what was motivating them before the meeting tonight.

He breakfasted on V-8 juice and vitamins, washed his

hands after smearing the Rogaine on, and walked down to his office. He started to call Slim, then remembered he was haying and wouldn't be available by phone. He dialed Senator Cline's office in Washington D.C. A woman's voice answered.

"Senator Cline's office. How may I help you?"

"Virginia—this is Hawk Neilson in Rapid City. Is the Senator in?"

"He is Mr. Neilson but he's in conference."

"Do you remember the name of the guy we dealt with at the Bureau of Indian Affairs last year?"

"Dan Hogue?"

"That's right. Do you have his number?"

"Sure. It's 348-9293."

"Thanks. Ask Senator Cline to call me when he gets a moment please."

Hawk dialed the number and waded through the voice mail options until a soft voice said, "Dan Hogue."

"Dan—this is Hawk Neilson in Rapid City, Idaho. You probably don't remember me but I met you with Senator Cline when we were reviewing a proposed land exchange which included the Nez Perce."

The voice was even. "I remember you Mr. Neilson."

"Dan—has the tribe kept you up with their goals in this transaction? It is going to close this Friday and we're having the final meeting with them tonight and I just wondered if you were abreast of the probable outcome. What they are giving up and what they are getting?"

"Oh—I think so—yes. Have you talked with them lately?"

"What do you mean by lately?"

"Since Cruit Johnson entered the picture?"

Hawk cleared his throat. "Why? Has that changed the course for some reason?"

"Well—I'm not one to disclose a trust position but I think it would be incumbent on you to have a talk with them very soon—certainly before…"

"I intend doing just that—tonight—but I was hoping you could shed some light on their current thinking."

"What I want to say, Mr. Neilson, is that the BIA will most likely approve the terms of the exchange if the Indians are fully behind it. The exchange must come to us with approval by all parties."

"Of course. Well—thank you for your time Dan."

"Your welcome Mr. Neilson—and good luck."

Good luck? What the hell made him say that? We've been three years on this thing and he is just now wishing me good luck! Sometimes I wish I was back on the farm. I could be through milking now—looking out over the valley watching the sun come up instead of calling Washington DC before the crows move out of the hills here.

6:30 a.m. Tuesday, June 9, 1998

He took out his checkbook and looked at the balance. This was bill-paying day. He would be short so he concentrated on who to pay and who to extend. He hated writing checks. It was a clerk's job, not his, but today it fell on him. He took the list of accounts payable and wrote checks for those he absolutely had to pay. Sue Diggs--$2,200. He almost wrote on the stub 'for cooking my meals, massages, washing my clothes, and occasional sex' but thought better of it.

She just has to make some deals of her own—help support herself.

He signed it. He didn't have time to deal with that right now.

The phone rang as he finished.

"Jefferson County Realty," he answered.

"Hawk—Senator Cline in sunny Washington D.C.— what's up on the river?"

"Hi Frank. Thanks for calling back. I just talked to Dan Hogue at BIA and he not only isn't telling me anything from the Indians point of view, he is saying that their goals have changed since Cruit Johnson came to town. You know anything about that?"

"No, Hawk—I don't. Let me make a few calls and see what I can dig up. I'll get back to you."

"We have a dinner meeting at 5:00 with the Indians, so see if you can get back to me before I go in there without a game plan and get scalped."

"It's almost 11 o'clock here now—I'll get back to you before 3:00 p.m. my time."

"Appreciate that Frank."

"It's the least I can do for a loyal constituent. Keep sending your donations."

"I just paid bills. I'm broke."

"You'll make more one of these days."

8:00 a.m. Tuesday, June 9, 1998

Hawk entered by the back door. George Arbuckle was the only person there.

"Hawk—glad you're here early. The hotel tried to run the credit card yesterday and it was rejected. What do we do now?"

Hawk was silent for a moment.

Damn that kid!

He handed George another credit card. "See if this will fly."

"Ok, but it's pretty embarrassing to me when they tell me it won't…."

"You—what about me—it's my card!"

Damn that kid!

George left for the hotel. Hawk stood and opened his mail while he listened to his voice mail messages. Nothing from the IRS yet. That was good. If he could stall them until after the closing he would have time for them, for reading, for a vacation, for remodeling the patio on his house, for retirement. He opened a notice from the Visa account.

Dear account holder

Your account #2335-3444-6868 is past due.
Please remit payment immediately in enclosed envelope
or call our offices at 800-928-6758. Failure to do so
may endanger your account status.

Damn that kid!

He dialed Carroll Swenson's private number at the bank.

"Good morning Hawk."

"Does everybody have caller ID in this country?"

"Just the endangered species," Carroll said.

"Carroll—will you get me a cashier's check for $5,000.
Make it out to Citibank Visa."

"Which account do you want me to overdraw?"

"Come on Carroll—there must be enough in there to
cover that."

"I'll tell you something. The deposits in this bank are
less by $120,000 this morning. Your transaction account has
only a hundred dollars left in it."

"What the hell happened?"

"Draft to Wells Fargo Bank for $120,000."

"When?"

"This morning."

"Judas H. Priest…"

"Indeed…that and more," Carroll said.

"Will you cover me on the five grand? I just delivered
you a check for $75,000," Hawk pleaded.

"Till when?"

"Friday."

"My gawd…I hope the world doesn't come to an end.
We've got too much riding on Friday."

Hawk held his breath.

"Ok—till Friday at 3:00 p.m.," Carroll said.

"Thanks Carroll."

"Don't thank me. Thank the guy that comes after me
and unravels all this stuff."

"Aw Carroll—you're talking like a fatalist."

"I'm a realist, Hawk. A cotton pickin' realist. Come over and pick it up in an hour."

Hawk looked through the glass walls into the main office. Wev and RuthAnn had arrived. Hawk bolted out of his chair and grabbed the doorknob. He held it for a second thinking of how to open the conversation, trying to control his breathing and himself.

"RuthAnn—could I see you for a minute please?"

She shot a quick glance at Wev, straightened her skirt and walked toward Hawk's office.

"Grab the Transaction Account checkbook please," Hawk said.

She continued into his office and sat down. He closed the door and stood holding the doorknob for a few seconds, looking at her back. She faced his empty chair, shoulders straight, erect in her posture.

Showdown stance. I'd know that position anywhere.

"RuthAnn—why didn't you bring in the checkbook like I asked?" Hawk said.

"There is no reason to bring it in."

"Why is that?"

"There's no money in it."

Hawk walked to his chair and sat down. "I just became aware of that."

The one who speaks first loses. I've got to hold my tongue until she says something. Thirty seconds passed.

"Do you have something you want to say?" Hawk said.

"No."

"RuthAnn--$120,000 got transferred to Wells Fargo Bank. Did you do that?"

"Yes."

"And just why was that?"

"I felt it was safer there."

"Safer from what?"

"You."

"Me?" Hawk twisted in his chair.

"Yes."

Another thirty seconds passed. She was calm and he had to remain so.

"I want it put back in our bank today—now."

She shook her head.

He jumped up from his seat and stormed over to her desk. "Where's the checkbook?"

She turned and looked at him. "There is no checkbook for the new account."

"Where are the counter checks—they had to give you some checks?"

"Here in my purse."

Wev watched as he walked very fast back into his office and grabbed her purse. He rummaged through it and found the envelope with six counter checks, threw the purse into her lap and sat down. He wrote out a check for $120,000 and signed it.

"This will close that account," he said.

RuthAnn had a partial smile on her face. "No it won't."

"Why not?"

"You're not an authorized signer on the account."

"I'm the President of this company…"

"…I am the Treasurer and authorized to open and close accounts and sign checks."

He sat stunned. "Get the hell out of my office—NOW!"

She uncrossed her legs, stood up and walked back to her desk. Wev's eyes were as big as billiard balls. By that time, Stoddard Greening and George Arbuckle were in the office and the normal hum of activity was catching up with the tension.

Hawk stood up—anger building within him. He picked up the checks, strode out to RuthAnn and flung them on her desk.

"Make one out for $120,000 and sign it," he said.

She shook her head.

"RuthAnn—if you don't sign that I'm calling a corporation meeting in fifteen minutes and you know who owns most of the stock. I'm replacing you and Wev and putting that money under my control. Then I'm filing a law suit against you for conversion of funds, and a stockholders suit against you for failure to act responsibly with company money, and a personal lawsuit for ruining my credit…and creditability."

She looked at him but did not move.

"Wev—talk some sense into her. She's ruining me," Hawk pleaded.

"It's our money too," Wev said.

"Your money—hell. What have you put into this deal?"

"Hawk—we've been working on it for three years just like you have."

"When did you leave town and sleep in lousy motels and eat lousy food and meet with ranchers at six in the morning or ten at night or fly to Boise or Washington to meet with Fish & Wildlife or BLM or the BIA? Never…that's when!"

He was out of breath and didn't wait for an answer. Red faced, he pivoted on his left foot, lowered his shoulder putting his entire body weight behind the punch and drove his fist into the wall. The sheetrock cratered—powder flew from the gap. It was nailed to a 2x4 that cracked like a rifle shot. There was not a sound in the room—everyone frozen wide eyed, open mouthed. Hawk did not trust himself to speak. He stomped out of the room, ran down the stairs and into the alleyway. When he crossed Idle Street he slowed to a walk. By that time his wrist, hand, and fingers were the size of his knee. He walked to Sue's house. She took him to the emergency room.

1:00 p.m. Tuesday, June 9, 1998

The bandage reached from the tip of his fingers to mid forearm. It throbbed clear up to Hawk's shoulder, each heart beat increasing the sick feeling in his stomach.

"You want to go back to the office?" Sue said.

"No. Take me home," Hawk said. "No—wait. Take me by the bank."

At the bank Hawk picked up the cashiers check, borrowed a clean envelope and mailed it with the late notice to Visa.

"Ok—now take me home."

"You know," Sue began. "Tearing doors off the hinges and smashing walls isn't going to make an impression on Ruthann."

"Sue—this is not a good time to discuss this."

"I know, but this time you'll listen cause I'm driving."

They rounded the corner and crossed the railroad tracks. Sue waved at the gas station attendant. She continued up the river grade and turned into the driveway.

"I'll make you some lunch," she said and followed him in.

Sue dug through the left overs and put together some roast turkey sandwiches, ice-tea and carrots. The carrots were limp; so was the lettuce.

"Do you ever eat anything out of here that I get you?" she asked.

"Not much."

"You need a goat. She'd eat your leftovers and you could get the milk. Be good for you."

"I'd just have to hire someone to milk the damn thing."

The phone rang and Sue answered it. She handed the phone to Hawk. "It's Senator Cline."

"Hello Senator.

"Hawk…I haven't got much, but the jist of the rumor mill is that there is a big push to get back ancestral lands. You know—hunting, fishing, burial grounds—that sort of thing. Maybe even to the exclusion of what might get them more cash flow such as the commercial lands that could come to them from this exchange you've drafted. I…"

"Senator—cutting this deal up now is gonna kill it. I've already got one rancher who holds a good part of that sort of land not wanting to do it."

"Who's that?"

"Slim Collins."

"He'll come along in the final analysis won't he? I mean…"

"Who knows? Talks like he will only trade for high meadow country. Something up around Buffalo Lake."

"I don't think BLM will even consider doing that—do you?"

"No."

Senator Cline coughed. "This weather in Washington DC stinks. Why they decided to put the capital here is more than I…"

"Have you got any clout with BLM?" Hawk inserted.

"I know some of the people down there. We've had a few meetings with them—and some about this deal…but clout? I don't know—I doubt it."

"Can you get one of your aides to plumb their true feelings about Buffalo Lake and get back to me ASAP?"

"I can put Dick Mulder on it. He's got some legal training and he knows some of the guys and gals in BLM…yeah he'd be a good one. I'll ask him to get with them then call you when he's got some feelings under his belt."

"Great. Thanks Senator."

"Your welcome as always Hawk. The steelhead biting yet?"

"Not the size you like."

"Well—don't take all the big ones until I get back there."

"Got a boat, a bottle of Jack Daniels, and a split bamboo fly rod for you to try out."

"I'm on my way. So long Hawk."

Hawk handed the phone to Sue.

Chapter 7

2:00 p.m. Tuesday, June 9, 1998

Hawk wolfed down four Tylenol with milk. After the pain subsided he sat in the living room looking out over the river and turned off every thought except for the Indians. He started with a mental picture of the last meeting. Each face, all twelve chairs filled with tribal members, the light bouncing off the walls so he could see their expressions, if they had any, and the shuffling of feet, rustling of paper, an occasional cough amidst the muted talk. The pervading dusty salty odor of country men. There had to be a way to see behind their stoic wall, he knew it; he believed it.

Senator Cline had mentioned the historic position of the original people, the hunting, fishing, and burial grounds. Was that it? Or was it cover for what they really wanted?

He turned around. Sue was standing in the archway to the patio. He looked at her and remembered the moves she had made on the couch last night. He just realized how much he would miss her if she wasn't there. She filled in the blank spots in his life and not with just detail and cooking and sex. She was not an object—she was a workmate and anytime he reached back he could touch her or see something she had done. They worked together like a pair of horses in harness, each giving assistance from their efforts to the other. It was getting so he wanted to see her when he awoke in the mornings. He needed to start sorting things out after this deal. His life could be changing while he wasn't paying attention to it.

"What?" he said.

She smiled and put one foot up on the bench. "When do you want to talk about what I need?"

"Need—like what need?"

"Like money to pay my bills."

"I pay you that now."

"It isn't covering it."

Hawk twisted in the chair. "Well—it can wait until Fri…"

"No it can't Hawk. I need it tomorrow."

"Tomorrow?"

"I need to pay some bills."

"Tell them to hold off. Next week."

"You pay your bills, why can't I pay mine?"

"I didn't pay all of them. Only necessary ones."

Sue thought for a moment. "Ok. I only need $2,000 then."

"For crying out loud—you think I've got two grand lying around when I can't even pay my bills. I've got an account at the café for more than that and I just paid you two thousand…"

"Hawk—we've talked about this before. You always bring up your bills, your accounts—that this deal is going to make us all wealthy. I've strung these people along as far as I can. I've got to have money."

"Dammit Sue…." The throbbing in his arm started again. He raised it over his head to ease it. "Type up a check. I can probably float it until Friday."

Sue smiled and looped a warm arm around his neck. "You're a good man Hawk."

The phone rang and Hawk took it with his left hand. The throbbing was stronger now.

"Hawk Neilson here."

"Hawk—you old son of a gun—you still alive?"

"Not all of me. Who's this?"

"Kellogg"

"Rusty Kellogg?"

"For sure it is. Just this minute had a hankering to call you."

Hawk smiled at his mental picture of Rusty Kellogg. "You still in San Jose, still married to the prettiest girl in California, and still the wealthiest guy in your club?"

"Yes, yes, and no."

"Some wealthier guy moved into your area huh?"

There was a moment of silence. "No Hawk. Money doesn't mean much sometimes. It won't buy health, and health can be the real measure of wealth."

"It bought me a back surgeon and an eye surgeon," Hawk said.

"Yeah? Well—I've got macular degeneration, the wet kind, and I could throw money at it all day long and I'd still be virtually blind."

"My God, Kellogg. You could spot a deer a mile away."

"No more. Can't read the paper, can't drive, can't see TV. Mine's a world of can't's now."

"You sound morbid." Hawk heard him cough.

"No—I'm not. Just down a little. It's hard to retire with

everything made, everything working so well and then have this hit you. Doesn't strike me as fair."

"You remember how often we discussed the fairness in this world...."

"Oh I know. Really didn't call to tell you my troubles but I wanted you to know why I'm not returning your e-mails. Can't read the computer screen anymore. Didn't want you to think I was ignoring you."

"I'm sorry Kellogg."

"Yeah—I know." He sighed audibly. "Hope your life is going ok."

"Pretty good—right now pretty good." He looked at Sue who had come back onto the patio with the check in her hand. He could see the house and the river and the sunshine filtering through the trees in the front yard. "Pretty good. Working hard on closing a deal this Friday but it'll go. Busted my hand on a wall, but other than that...."

"Kids doing ok?"

"You know the kids. One's too straight to get into trouble and the other one's too crooked to stay out of trouble."

Kellogg paused a minute. "Life. What a deal huh?"

"I wouldn't have missed it for anything, would you?"

"Naw. Put it all together and I'd have chosen what I did. I'll learn to live with this thing. Just wanted you to know. I'll call you more often."

"I'd like that. Call next week after this deal closes. No—I'll call you."

"Ok. I'll wait for your call. So long Hawk."

He laid the receiver down and rested his hand on it. He lifted his eyes to air that was startlingly clear, ripples finding their way downstream near the far bank of the river. There was an osprey on the fourth limb up in the bull pine tree on the near bank. What a joy to be alive and fit and neck deep into a battle that you believe in and determined to win. To have the motivation and the ability; the true joy of living when less fortunate people crossed his path every day. Kellogg—almost blind. His eyes were moist, he lifted his head and whispered. "Oh God— let me see the sun one more time."

"What?" Sue said.

Hawk turned his head, looked down, looked at the grass. "Kellogg—an old classmate of mine." He paused. "He married the prettiest girl in California, got wealthy, and now he's going blind."

Her eyes visibly saddened. "I'm sorry," she said.

Hawk took a deep breath, then let it out through his nose. "Yeah—me too." He reached up and touched her hand. She held it and put her other hand on his shoulder.

"You ok?"

He nodded. Had anyone driven by and glanced up the gentle rise they would have looked like a couple with years of understanding behind them. The afternoon air was hot and moist with bird sounds drifting up from the river. It was a good day to be alive.

He signed the check and handed it to her.

3:00 p.m. Tuesday, June 9, 1998

For a while after Sue left, Hawk dozed in the lounge chair. His mind contrived to keep him from total sleep while it hatched his plan; a process he had used for years. Throw the knowns into a pile and then let his unconscious sort it out and give him an answer. He often wondered how the solution to a problem drifted unrealized in his mind until he gave it up from his conscious mind. Then he would find it as an idea that he could develop and sculpt.

He actually had three layers here. The Indians presumably, wanted ancestral lands which Slim owned. Slim wanted late summer pasture that BLM owned. BLM and Fish & Game wanted the water front but wouldn't give up a chunk of high country pasture on Buffalo Lake to get it. Everybody had signed preliminary agreements but nothing was truly binding. And now—enter Cruit Johnson whose wife is living with Jonathan and the BIA guy deferring to the tribe on this—at least for now.

A surge of pain hit him as he elbowed himself upright in the chair. He had forgotten about his hand.

"Judas-H-Priest!" he yelled. He fell back into the chair. A bead of sweat broke out on his upper lip and forehead. He mopped it with his left hand.

What a way to go into the meeting—my arm in a sling. What I need to show is courage and confidence and commitment. I can't even shake hands. How do you make a peace treaty with the Nez Perce and not shake hands? Smoke a pipe; give them a gift? There isn't a gift that they would appreciate that I can afford. Besides, I don't want them thinking I'm buying this deal. Make it on the merits like you have all the other deals. It's a good one for everybody.

It was a mantra for him. He'd repeated it in a hundred motel rooms where he'd spent countless hours and days putting this exchange together. It had to work for everyone. Whenever a piece didn't work it had to be removed and another piece inserted. Somebody had the piece of real estate that was needed; all he had to do was find it. Read the maps, scour the County Court Houses, find the owners, drive sixty miles to talk to them and don't let them get the idea that their piece is the linchpin for the whole deal. He could recall the sheer joy of getting a piece in the puzzle and feeling the satisfaction of the owner looking forward to the new ownership. He had felt it maybe three hundred times over the years, but the buzz was still there. The creeping smile that loosened the tension of the face to face discussion, then the handshake and the nodding that the owner usually did, being glad to have it over with. Or if it was an agency, seeing the officer walk back to his office taller, straighter, having made his agency more efficient and thus more capable of completing their mission of land management.

He looked at his watch. He had a little over an hour to get to the meeting.

4:45 p.m. Tuesday, June 9, 1998

    Jonathan drove his pickup into the hotel parking lot. It had been one of the slickest pickups in town, midnight black, flames painted on the side, an antenna that stuck up ten feet above the cab. It had been outfitted with large chrome wheels and hubcaps so polished that you could see the color of your eyes in them. Hawk glanced at the replacement wheels.

    "Dad—could I see you a minute?"

    Hawk squinted into the late afternoon sun.

    "What'd you do to your hand?" Jonathan said.

    "What do you want?" Hawk said. "You coming in?"

    "Hell no. I don't want Cruit to see me here."

    "You failed to mention that his wife was living with you."

    "For damn good reason," Jonathan said.

    Hawk shifted his stance. "He may crucify me because of that. And kill the deal."

    Jonathan nodded. He reached behind the seat and brought out an object wrapped in newspaper. It was long and slightly heavy at one end.

    "I traded for this yesterday. I think it's authentic. Thought you might use it some way to get the Indians to go along."

    "What is it?" Hawk said.

    "Take a look…."

    "I can't open it with this hand."

    Jonathan started to unwrap it and Hawk said; "Traded what for it?"

    "Does it matter, Dad?" His eyes pierced Hawk's, the youthful smile gone, replaced by a serious face, showing wrinkles even in the failing light. He finished unwrapping and laid the pipe with two attached eagle feathers in his father's outstretched hand.

    The redstone bowl was black and brown from the stains

of many smokes. The eagle feathers danced in the slight breeze. Hawk starred at it.

"Jonathan…this…this is an old piece."

"Something was said about it belonging to Chief Joseph."

"I can't take this," Hawk said shaking his head.

"The guys I got it from—the people—they got value for it."

"It's not that—it's…"

"Dad. Take it and give it back to them. It could help your deal."

Jonathan wrapped it up in the paper and handed it to Hawk. Hawk didn't reach for it so Jonathan grabbed Hawk's elbow and lifted his arm, stuck the pipe between his arm and his body and gently lowered his arm over it.

The undersize worn out tires on steel rims squealed as the pickup turned onto the main road.

Those tires won't last long either.

Hawk found the conference room. He hid the pipe behind the wall table where the refreshments were going to be laid out. Then he poured himself a glass of ice water, laid out his notes and sat in the chair.

He knew exactly where to start with this thing. Start with the land history of the area, point to the past problems with all the ownerships and how this transaction, crafted with over 130 private parties, BLM, Fish and Wildlife, Forest Service, and the Nez Perce tribal lands, would lead to a better future for all parties. Then open it to questions? Had to. He had to be careful that he didn't let Cruit Johnson take over the meeting. In the old days Cruit wouldn't have thought of it, but he hadn't seen him for years. Cruit hanging up on him the other night didn't look like a good omen.

At exactly 5:00 p.m. the Indians filed in and took seats. They looked straight ahead and crossed their arms over their chests. One seat was left vacant at the far end of the table facing Hawk's chair.

So, they scouted it out.

Stoddard Greening and George Arbuckle came in and sat next to Hawk. They nodded to Hawk who was running his eyes over the Indians trying to determine where the problems could come from.

Then Cruit came through the door, walked to the one vacant seat and stood behind it looking up and down both sides of the table. Even though he wore loose clothing, the material seemed to mold to his body flowing over his broad shoulders to his narrow waist. Two braids starting in the middle of his head hung down his back, swinging when he moved. Physically he was still impressive although his handsome face was lined and his jowls sagged a bit. He nodded to Hawk and sat down.

"Hello Cruit," Hawk said. "Good to see you back in town."

Cruit nodded.

Oh—it's going to be a silent game huh?

"I want to introduce Stoddard and George here, whom I think you know. Let me bring out the points for this meeting then we can have some food and talk about it. I'd appreciate it if you would hold any questions until I get through my presentation.

"Starting with the gold strike and the general westward migration of the…"

Tell them what you're going to tell them; tell them; then tell them what you told them. That had worked in the past and it was the skeleton upon which Hawk hung every presentation. True—he had asked them to hold their questions until he was through, but it seemed—no felt—like what he was saying was not being understood. He knew most of these guys, had gone to school with several of them. They knew and understood English very well.

He finished, the food was brought in and everybody filled a plate then sat back down at the table. He heard the

Indians speaking only Nez Perce. When the plates were cleaned and pushed to the center of the table Cruit Johnson stood up. He stood behind his chair, hands gripping the top rung.

"Hawkins Neilson—good to see you. Thank you for this meeting and for the food you have provided. We know Stoddard Greening and George Arbuckle." He nodded to them.

"Your plan will not work." He paused. "It provides the Nez Perce with nothing we don't already have. We are not interested in more of the same. You talk about development. Stores, gas stations, lodges, but we have land for that if we choose to use it that way. More reservation land doesn't fulfill us. What else can you offer?"

"What do you mean—what else? You're getting a good tra...."

"Good value for trade—yes—but not what we <u>want</u> in trade!" Cruit said.

"What could you want <u>more</u> than productive land with commercial enterprises or more farm and ranch land—it would provide jobs for your people, cash income, help build schools, health centers, recreation centers...."

Cruit was shaking his head even as he interrupted. "Not what we want now. We want ancestral lands. Where our people traditionally hunted, fished, picked fruit and berries, and buried our dead. These lands we want back into our tribe—we want to be a whole people again. There was a time we wanted to be like white men but no more. We want the lands along the river that Slim Collins claims.

"That's going to Fish & Game for salmon...." Hawk started.

"We know where it is going and why. But if you research it carefully, you will find that our ancestors used that land for thousands of years. We netted fish. The buffalo crossed the river there. Our ancestors went to the spirits amongst those trees. That is the land we want back for what we are giving up. If you can return it to us in this trade—this transaction you call it—then we will sign. If not—the meeting is over." Cruit sat down. In one orchestrated move, the Indians turned and looked at Hawk.

The alternatives were flying in his head like arrows at a wagon train. This was Tuesday…he couldn't get Fish & Game to…and Slim…he was haying and couldn't be reached…where was there anything else to throw in? Who the hell did they think they were…this was a bonanza for the tribe…a friggin gold mine…BIA would surely not agree to this proposal… would they? Could they if the Indians insisted?

"That's crazy—that's the craziest thing I ever heard of!" Hawk said.

"What's crazy about it?" Cruit said.

"You can't earn any money on that land. It's only good for pasture and water. Why don't you take what's offered—develop it, get an income and buy what you want?"

"Too long we tried that. We are not good managers of businesses."

"You can provide schools…"

"What good will that do?"

"Look what it did for you," Hawk said, his voice rising.

"I got my education in prison—from white man's prison—and now we want to live our lives our way, not your way or the BIA's way or any missionary's way—our way!"

"You can't…"

"Don't tell us what we can and can't do Hawk—we're through with that!"

Hawk could feel the thin threads holding the transaction together breaking as the requirements changed, moved around, danced in the heat of the day on the bank of the river. He blinked. His arm was pounding. He swallowed then clamped his tongue between his teeth. Judas H. Priest! I'm swimming—nothing to grab hold of—nothing but water and sky. Where's your confidence, your commitment, your courage?

Hawk jammed his good hand down on the table and levered himself up. "Let me see what I can do."

The Indians stood up en masse and filed out the door.

"Cruit—could I see you a minute?" Hawk said.

Don't open any old wounds. Give him the pipe and get it off your conscience.

Hawk, using his left hand, pulled the pipe from under the table.

"I want you to have this."

Cruit hefted it and looked in Hawk's eyes. The paper fell away and he held the ancient pipe in his hands. He stroked a feather then lifted the bowl to his nose and inhaled. He held it in both hands like a soldier presenting a sword to an officer and looked at it while his eyes misted. He spoke softly. "It is very old."

"Someone said it could have belonged to Chief Joseph."

Cruit nodded. "Very possibly—very possibly." He turned the pipe over in his hands. "Why are you giving me this?"

"It belongs with your people," Hawk said.

Cruit leveled his eyes and squinted. "So does that land on the river."

"Is that a must?"

"That is an absolute."

Hawk massaged his forearm above the bandage.

Cruit looked at the cast. "I heard you broke the 2x4. You still pack a punch."

"Cruit—why'd you hang up on me the other night at the Vet's Club?"

A smile crept across Cruit's face and lighted his eyes and as he rolled the pipe in his hands and stroked it, he said, "Good night Hawk."

Chapter 8

6:35 a.m. Wednesday, June 10, 1998

At the restaurant Ella held the coffee pot over Hawk's head. "With or without cream?"

"I'd like it in the cup if it isn't too much trouble," he said.

"See your name in the paper?"

"No...why?"

"You'll see it. Cruit's in there too."

Hawk went through all twelve pages and found it under the LOCAL section, a picture of Cruit holding the pipe out-stretched in his hands like he had taken it last night, no smile on his face but his nostrils flared like he was holding in his emotions. The headlines read:

--Chief Joseph Pipe Returned to Tribe—

Cruit Johnson, local Nez Perce representative received an anonymous return of a pipe reported to have belonged to Chief Joseph through the offices of Hawkins Neilson last night at a meeting in the Hotel Del Rey.

The pipe has been missing from a museum collection for several years, and has been the object of a statewide search. Local police are mum on whether they intend to take possession of the pipe or leave it with the tribe.

Mr. Johnson said the tribe will place the pipe in a place of honor on the reservation and it will be available for anyone to see it at the Chief Joseph Museum that is being built in the old Frontier Store building near the post office.

"Nice photo of the lad," Thaddeus Burton said as he slid into the booth. "Doesn't look too worse for the wear."

"Since when are you an expert on wear?" Hawk said.

"Since my divorce three years, four months, eleven days and…" he looked at his watch, "…two hours from now. My expert advice is constantly sought by those less fortunate than myself."

Hawk chuckled. "Are there some around?"

"The streets are running over with them." Thaddeus raised his arm. "Coffee please Ella."

Carroll Swenson came and slid in with them.

"I didn't know bankers got up this early," Thaddeus said.

"Have to to stay ahead of you guys." Carroll nodded at the paper. "How'd you get hold of the pipe?

"Someone left it for me—said it should go back to the Indians," Hawk said.

"Anyone we know?" Thaddeus said, lifting his eyebrows.

"Left it on my porch in the dead of night wrapped in a newspaper. Had a note with it."

"Oh. How exciting." Thaddeus bubbled. "Didn't try to burn down your house or anything?"

"Seems to me, it appeared at a strange time," Carroll said. "This is Wednesday and you're closing the deal which includes the Indians on Friday. Why would someone return it so timely unless they were using the act for some purpose?"

Hawk straightened up and looked down his nose at his contemporaries. "Someone chooses me to return the pipe and right away you guys are suspicious."

"Seems that way," Thaddeus said.

"How's it looking, Hawk?" Carroll said.

"Pretty good. Some loose ends to tie up but we'll close it Friday come hell or high water."

"Could you drop by the bank before you go to the office, Hawk? Something I'd like to discuss with you," Carroll said.

"You can say anything here—Thaddeus knows all of my warts."

"Does he know about the Boise matter?"

"Of course. He's the one that's gonna keep me out of jail if I'm wrong," Hawk said.

"The IRS put a lien on your account—your personal account—just before closing last night."

"What's that got in it—a dollar eighty-five?" Hawk said.

"Not much—you're right." Carroll dropped his voice. "But it doesn't look good for one of our directors to have his account levied."

"Well Carroll, there's not much I can do about that. My legal team together with my professional accounting team will just have to clear that matter up." He sipped his coffee.

"You're treating this pretty cavalier."

"Carroll," Thaddeus said, as he held up his forefinger in mock admonishment, "Say nothing to the rest of your board about this matter. I must protect the integrity of my client and he is innocent until proven guilty before a court of law. I hereby request, on behalf of my client, that you make no further mention of this to anyone, living or dead."

"For Christ's sake Thad, I'm just saying it looks…"

"I know. It's just so early in the morning to get serious. Drink your coffee and count your rosary beads again."

Hawk finished the paper and folded it on the table. "Nothing in here about either of you guys—so who's buying the coffee? My account's been levied. I'm outta here."

8:05 a.m. Wednesday, June 10, 1998

Stoddard spun around in his chair when Hawk entered the office.

"Morning Hawk. What ever happened to that piece of property Royal Cunningham used to own back up near the pass?"

"Damned if I know. He was talking about logging it but I don't think he did."

"He still owns it?" Stoddard said.

"As far as I know. Call him—he'll tell you."

Stoddard rolled his lip between his teeth. "I was just thinking—that could be our missing piece."

"How so?" Hawk said.

"Well—we offer that to Slim in exchange for his river front and give the river front to the Indians for their ancestral requirements."

"Yeah—and that leaves us buying Cunningham's land for money which we haven't got in this transaction," Hawk replied.

"Think about it Hawk. It could be the answer. I'll call Cunningham and see what's up with that property."

Hawk dialed the IRS office in Boise.

"You have reached the voice mail for David Bires. Please leave a message at the beep."

"Morning David. This is Hawk Neilson. My banker tells me you have levied my account and I…"

"Good morning Mr. Neilson," Bires cut in. "Sorry, I was on the other line and heard your message and picked up. How may I help you today?"

"My banker tells me you levied my account—all $1.85 of it. I thought you were sending papers and we'd go at this like gentlemen, but you've jumped that line and are playing hardball. If you think you can squeeze and get something you are not entitled to, you're nuttier than a fruitcake. Number one; I don't squeeze, and two, I don't give, and three—I don't quit. You start with me and I'll have the congressman and both senators in your office tomorrow wondering why you didn't give a taxpayer a decent time frame to respond. You sent the stuff Monday and it is now Wednesday and it hasn't arrived yet."

"Please be calm Mr. Neilson. There must be some mistake."

"You damn right there is and I want it corrected this morning—before noon."

"What is it you want corrected?"

"I want that levy lifted as soon as we hang up." Hawk said.

"I did not place a levy on your account."

"Well someone did—it came from your office, so get rid of it. There is supposed to be a thirty day notice before any levy—you know it and I know it."

"Sounds like you have dealt with the IRS before Mr. Neilson."

"I have an attorney who knows this stuff."

"I'll find out about it and get back to you," Bires said.

"Get back to me—HELL—I want that levy lifted before noon. You got that?" Hawk slammed down the receiver.

Stoddard Greening was standing in the doorway to Hawk's office, his lips pursed. Hawk looked at him, took a deep breath and sat upright in his chair.

"Not good for your blood pressure," Stoddard said.

"To hell with my blood pressure!"

"Hawk—Cunningham says he still has that 360 acres and he'd be willing to listen to any deal we have. He'll be around today and tomorrow but after that he'll be gone for two weeks."

"Lovely—fucking lovely," Hawk said.

"Hawk—calm down please. There's no need for you to start swearing and getting agitated. I think this could work. We need to approach this with reason and intelligence."

"That's your suit Stoddard. I'm the Full Speed Ahead Damn the Torpedoes partner…remember?"

"Ok—ok. Just give me a couple of hours to work on it."

Hawk stood up and put on his jacket.

"Where you going?" Stoddard asked.

"Someone needs to talk to Fish and Game. If they don't get the river frontage, what do they get out of this deal? And BLM—they don't get rid of that rock and rattlesnake land—Judas Priest, the whole thing is falling down around our necks and the Indians are smoking the peace pipe."

Stoddard held up his hand. "Hold it Hawk. There is a way out of this, it just takes some thought."

"Well—I'm not thinking very good right now."

"You gonna drive while you're that mad?" Stoddard said.

"Well I'm sure as hell not gonna walk."

Hawk stepped through the doorway not looking to right or left. Wev and Ruth Ann looked up from their desks, their faces like stone. George Arbuckle glanced up in the mirror over his desk to watch Hawk stamp across the room. The door closed. The silence was deafening.

8:30 a.m. Wednesday, June 10, 1998

Hawk pulled into the parking lot and shut off the engine. He was churning the IRS lien over in his mind, his heart pounding, his gut tight. The building he was staring at he had built twenty years ago and leased to the Idaho Fish & Game department. A few trophy heads, some outstanding mounted steelhead, and a huge map of Idaho filled the entry. They didn't take good care of the trophies so it always smelled like an animal warehouse. It was one of the first properties he had sold Royal Cunningham. With the cash he had financed his first big exchange which started him on his new career of solving everybody's problem with someone else's property. He was up to his nose in this deal now. Fish & Game had to go along. There were no other players to substitute. He pushed the car door open, sat for a minute in the seat with one foot on the ground, took three deep breaths and stood up. He blinked several times—a little woozy.

Stoddard could be right. Anger does funny things to your body and your mind.

"Mr. Neilson—what can we do for you today?" the Fish & Game clerk said.

"Is Brad in?" Hawk said.

"He sure is. I'll get him."

Hawk helped himself to a cup of coffee and looked at the animal and fish mounts adorning the walls. He knew most of the hunters who had contributed the heads to the display. Some, that had been killed illegally, had been confiscated from the rogue hunters. He knew them too.

"Come on back, Hawk," Brad said. "What gets you up this early?"

"Hell Brad—I've been up since 6 o'clock trying to figure out how to satisfy your outfit in this transaction."

"We're happy with the river frontage."

Hawk looked out the window. "Trouble is, the Indians want it. Say it's ancestral land—that they've used it for hunting, fishing, and burial grounds forever. BIA's going along with them on it too."

"I thought everybody was settled except for Slim."

Hawk nodded. "Thought so. Turns out Cruit Johnson has the Indians thinking another way."

"When did this happen?" Brad said.

"Last night at a little meeting I had with them."

"Saw the picture of Cruit holding the pipe. You give it to him?"

Hawk nodded.

Brad took a deep breath, clasped his hands behind his head and leaned back in his chair.

Hawk started. "Brad—if the Indians agreed to Fish & Game management terms on that section of the river, would that satisfy your department?"

"Might. I could run it by a few guys and see how it sets."

"Would you do that? And get back to me today?" Hawk said.

"Anything for an old classmate."

"Thanks."

"Is Edith coming back to town anytime soon?" Brad said.

"Why?"

"Well—now that I'm single again I was thinking of how we used to dance up a storm at the school dances and wondering since she was married to the second-best guy in our class, she might like a crack at the first-best."

"Meaning you?"

Brad nodded.

"She's free, white, and twenty-one Brad. You can call her. She's living in Boise."

"You don't mind?"

"Not a bit. Might be good for you to be properly tamed."

"I'll call you after I move this thing through the office, Hawk."

"Call me before 6:00—I've got a serious meeting at that time at my home office."

Chapter 9

10:00 a.m. Wednesday, June 10, 1998

When Hawk got back to the office Stoddard was waiting for him.

"I've been thinking…"

"Good that someone around here has," Hawk said.

Stoddard waited for Hawk to sit down.

"…that Slim would take the high country land Royal has—it's about an even trade—and the Indians get the river parcel. BLM has to settle for straightening out the lines on their Section 31 and no inholdings to mess with. Fish and Game is where I'm stumped. What are we gonna give them?"

"Have you thought of the other 130 land owners going through this mine field?"

"Well—yeah—I ran them through my head but you know more about them then I do. I was just thinking how to solve Slim's problem if the Indians insist on the river piece," Stoddard said.

"I just don't know. I can't even think about it right now. But it'll come to me."

Stoddard watched Hawk sitting in his chair. This scene had been repeated a thousand times since they started this involved land exchange over four years ago. Stoddard would think of a problem, a point to handle, and present it in his quiet judicial way. Hawk would hear him out, dismiss it from the immediate conversation, then let it percolate on the back burner until at some moment his subconscious thought processes weeded it out and threw out a solution that invariably he thought of as his. When it worked, he always assumed it would; when it didn't, he shoved it back into the process until a solution came that did work. Up until now, something had always worked.

Hawk eased out of the chair and opened the wooden cabinet doors that hid the blackboard. He wrote the main players on the left. In the middle he wrote what they were giving up and on the right what they were getting.

Indians	Hiway frontage land/ranch	River/ancestral land
BLM	timber land/rocks & snakes	better boundaries
Fish & Game	hill land/ farm land/grazing	feeder streams /habitat
Forest Service	timber land/grazing/farm	better boundaries/trees
130 Pvt Owners	various inholdings	better quality land
Slim	river frontage/pasture	late season pasture

Then he wrote down.

Royal C.   late season pasture $$$$$$$

He threw the chalk on his desk.

"We don't have any money in this deal," he said.

"We've got our profit," Stoddard said.

Hawk looked at him like he had just been reported insane by the local psychiatrist.

"Well—we could," Stoddard persisted. "We've got $24 million coming as our profit. We could stand to invest a little in the land…even after taxes we'd still have plenty…"

"We're not going to start buying our way into this deal. Besides—you have any idea how long Royal has been sitting on that high ground? The thing is covered with snow six months, muddy for three, and so high the cows need oxygen for the other three. I doubt Slim would even consider it."

"Well—he might."

"You ask him. I'm not going to insult his intelligence that much."

"Think I will," Stoddard said.

"You can't," Hawk said.

Stoddard turned around. "Why not?"

"He's haying on the lower bench and you can't reach him by phone."

"I could drive down there…"

Hawk thought a moment, then nodded. "You could."

Stoddard stood up then hesitated like he didn't exactly know which direction to go. He turned his head then his body and walked out.

Hawk took a deep breath and watched him go to his desk, gather up his briefcase and cell phone and walk out the back door to the parking lot.

"It might work," he said. "It just might work."

Hawk waited until RuthAnn was off the phone. He put

his hands on her desk and getting his face up close, asked her to go to lunch.

"Why?" she said.

"I want to discuss this banking business peacefully and professionally."

She thought about it a moment, "Ok."

"Good," he said. "We'll go over a little early."

He sat in his office looking at the blackboard. He found it hard to concentrate on the solutions. So many possibilities. But over the four or so years, he had convinced over 150 people to participate. Within the agencies, personnel had left during that time, but the heirs to the transaction were all agreed except for Slim and Cruit. Their hold out now created problems with Fish &Game. His stomach began to knot up. He leaned back in his chair and rubbed it. It felt like a stone covered with skin. He picked up the phone and dialed.

"Dr. Harrison's office, this is Julie speaking."

"Hi Julie," Hawk said. "Ask Doc to phone me in a prescription for my stomach. It's knotting up something fierce."

"I'd better let you talk to him Mr. Neilson."

Richard Harrison M.D. came on the phone. "What's up Hawk?"

"Stomach's hard as a stone. Can you call me in to Rexall?"

"If I call in one more prescription without seeing you someone will come down here and jerk my license to practice over the phone."

"You wouldn't learn any more by me sitting in your office," Hawk said. "My stomach hurts and feels like a stone."

"When did it start?"

"Just now."

"Otherwise you feel alright?"

"Hell yes."

"You having a lot of stress again?"

Hawk pictured him going through a checklist.

"Look Doc—I just need to get through Friday."

"You taking other medications?"

"Viagra."

"That all?"

"Scotch."

"How much?"

"Couple ounces."

"Every hour or every day?"

"Judas Priest—what is this, an inquisition?"

"You tried anything else?"

"No."

"Ok. But this is the last time. Come see me next week if it doesn't go away or comes back after Friday. I'll give you enough to last the weekend just in case your timing's off. I don't want you interrupting my golf game with your silly pains."

"You could use it as an excuse for your lousy score. Loss of concentration, switching back and forth between golf and medicine, you'll figure out how to use it."

"I have to think of a new one. I've used that one too often. I'll call it in right now; should be ready by noon."

"Thanks Doc."

11:30 a.m. Wednesday, June 10, 1998

Hawk stopped by RuthAnn's desk. "You Ready?"

She nodded. "Ok if Wev comes along?"

"I suppose. You ganging up on me?"

"No—he has to eat too," she snipped.

The three of them settled into the booth against the back wall near the kitchen entrance. The noise of the waitresses coming and going would cover their conversation. Wev and RuthAnn took one side, Hawk the other. They ordered and sat in silence for a minute.

"How's your hand, Hawk?" Wev said.

"I'll live."

"Looks sore," RuthAnn said.

"Swelling has gone down," Hawk put it in his lap.

This is something I need to do diplomatically. Try thinking like a woman for once and chose your words carefully. Don't get her antagonistic right off the bat, but lead the conversation. Start with the benefits to them.

"Have you thought of what you're going to do with your share of the profits?" Hawk said.

Wev and RuthAnn looked at each other.

"We've been thinking of a motor home. Doing some traveling," Wev said.

"Good. Good idea."

"And of course, the children's college. After that we haven't thought much about it," RuthAnn said.

Hawk nodded. "This is like a college degree, the culmination of four years of work. All coming down to commencement this Friday at the escrow office. You have all the documents down there, RuthAnn?"

"Yes. But I understand Royal Cunningham may be putting in some land and I don't have that done. Don't know what to prepare for that."

"Stoddard is suggesting our office put in the money to buy Royal's land and take some of the other stuff in the pot from the other owners or maybe that 640 acres BLM is trying to get rid of. I don't think that…"

"That's not something we should do," Wev said.

"Not should—but might have to," Hawk corrected.

"Well I don't think…" RuthAnn began.

Hawk held up his hand. "Don't spend time thinking about it right now—Stoddard just suggested it as a way of not having to go get some other piece to…"

"I'm against it," she said and crossed her arms.

The conversation stalled.

"That land is nothing but rocks and rattlesnakes," Wev said.

"I know, but it's worthless to BLM sitting in the middle of Slim's ranch and Slim has refused to take it."

"What the hell would we do with it?" Wev said.

"Maybe donate it to the Indians. He'd have a lot tougher time with them than with BLM. Could bring him around on the rest of the deal. Stoddard took off to track him down and see if he'll take Royal's high pass land. It might work."

Wev looked up. "Could we sell it to him on soft terms? Maybe $10,000 down and low interest for thirty years?"

"I doubt Slim would go into debt at this time in his life for that piece," Hawk said. He uses it now anyway, so owning it won't change his program any. We might get him to give us each a side of beef every year."

"I could live with that," RuthAnn said.

There was another lull while the food was delivered.

Hawk picked up his fork and poised it over his food. "RuthAnn—have you planned on paying the bills that are piling up today?"

She looked at Wev, then back at Hawk. "Some of them," she said.

Hawk's stomach bolted on him. He held off taking a bite. "Why only some of them?"

"Some seem high and are not backed up by the details for payment."

"Such as…?" Hawk said.

"I don't think we want to get into this now," she said.

Hawk put his fork down and put the bandaged hand on the table. This was the precise reason he had asked her to lunch. Now the stonewall.

"I have some reimbursements in that pile. I have credit card payments due, this restaurant, car payments…"

"I know all that, Hawk," she said.

Think like a woman, Hawk. Ferret this out, don't explode or hit anything. Question her nicely and evenly. Space it out and don't allow her to get mad. Give her a question she can't answer with a yes or no.

"How would you suggest I cover these while you are deciding what to do?"

She shrugged her shoulders. "Borrow from Carroll like you usually do until we get the money distributed."

"My credit line is tapped out," Hawk said.

"Oh I'm sure he'll help you out for a couple of days," she said.

"RuthAnn—I collected most of that money that's in the expense account. I got it from the agencies and timber companies and some of the ranchers. I got it and put it in that account."

"That's right." She took a bite and chewed it methodically. "However, I am the elected Treasurer and have been given authority to write the checks. You could have had it if you wanted it, but you don't write checks and you don't keep books and you don't do any of the little things that keep this organization running. You run around the countryside talking to people and running up expense accounts and expect me to pay them with little or no backup. You hand me a jumble of credit card receipts but you don't write who you had lunch or dinner with or why you stayed in a motel in Boise for two nights or where you went and why—and gas bills that would choke a giant corporation."

"If it wasn't for me we wouldn't be closing a $400 million deal on Friday," Hawk said.

"That's true," she said.

Hawk looked at Wev. In that instant he knew it wouldn't do a damn bit of good to bring him into the battle. He would support RuthAnn because he had to.

"RuthAnn—I need some support here. I can't be worrying about my bills and get this deal closed. I've got the Indians demanding the river property, Slim demanding high meadows, Royal demanding money..."

"Oh—you'll work it out. You always do."

Hawk shifted his body in the booth. "I need your help

here. In two days we close and we're each wealthy. Or it doesn't close and we're in debt up to our eyes."

"You've said that before."

"Of course—but it happens to be true. I'll take some time and specify the slips—can you…will you pay them then?"

"I always have haven't I?"

"Yes…with some teeth pulling."

"Hawk—I don't want those companies' auditors or the bank or IRS to come in and grill me on my books, and ask questions that…"

"They're not going to come…"

"You never know. If I keep a clean set of books I can sleep well at night. You're not dishonest, Hawk; you're just sloppy with details."

"That's what we've got you for."

"Precisely. And that is what I'm doing—details."

Hawk stopped. A pain grabbed his stomach so bad he bent over until his head touched the table.

Wev blanched. "What's the matter, Hawk?"

Hawk couldn't speak. His swollen hand held his stomach.

"You ok?" Wev said.

Hawk nodded. He stood up and threw his last twenty-dollar bill on the table and walked out.

At the Rexall Pharmacy he charged the prescription, went into the restroom and swallowed two of the pills before looking at the dosage printed on the label. *Take one tablet twice a day for stomach pain.* He washed them down with tap water and waited for the pain to go away. He thought of counting to see how long it took but looked in the mirror instead.

My god—aren't you a sorry sight? Busted hand; wolfing pills in a public restroom. What's to become of you, Hawkins Neilson? He shook his head. A jailhouse-lawyer Indian, a rancher with an 8th grade education, and your own employee have you dangling on a hook after forty-eight months of driving, negotiating, sweating, and stewing. And what has it gotten you? You're in debt up to your eyeballs, your stomach's being eaten away, your mistress requires a maintenance check every month...and it's Wednesday. What the hell does Wednesday have to do with it?

He laughed as the pain eased. "What a hoot," he said. "Wouldn't have missed it for anything."

Chapter 10

1:32 p.m. Wednesday, June 10, 1998

If it had happened in the middle of a town meeting it would not have passed through the population any faster. Hawk Neilson had grabbed his stomach and stormed out of the restaurant leaving his brother and sister-in-law in the booth. What do you suppose got into him this time?

"He needed a drink?"

"His girl friend called him on his cell phone?"

"That old football injury acting up?"

"Cruit Johnson called and said he was going to blow up Jonathan's trailer?"

Hawk heard it from six sources and gave each of them a different answer. They didn't have to know his guts were tied in a knot, the edges burning toward the middle. None of them had ever gone in the hole $1.2 million in expenses, and sat on the edge of a $24 million profit, then have the expected participants backslide, dance, wiggle, sideslip and squirm their way into another position three days before closing. It would be tough enough to close this thing the way it was written.

Hawk opened the large envelope with IRS in bold black letters on it.

Great—now everyone knows the IRS has a bone to pick with me. Yup...there are the forms. He dialed David Bires in Boise.

"Internal Revenue Service, David Bires speaking."

"Good afternoon David. This is Hawkins Neilson. I got your package with all the goodies in it. Did you remove the lien?"

"Hello Mr. Neilson. I'm working on that this minute."

Hawk counted to five. "How long will it take?" He tried to sound normal.

"I'm trying to find out who put it there. I just...."

"I'm not filling out any of this stuff until you remove it. It needs to be done today." He could hear Bires breathing. "Do I need to have my attorney call?"

"No sir. I'll get it cleared and I'll call you when it's done."

"Thank you Mr. Bires. Goodbye."

Hawk thought a moment then dialed Carroll at the bank.

"Carroll—when you and I were joking round this morning about my account being levied by the IRS...."

"How's the removal coming on that?" Carroll said.

"If you'd let me finish I will supply you with all the information you could possibly need, want, desire, and hope for."

"Sorry Hawk. Too much coffee."

"Anyway—we joked about them levying my personal account and it only having $1.85 in it. But I just remembered I put $75,000 in that account from the sale of property to Royal. Isn't that true?" Hawk said.

"Lemme check."

Hawk could hear the clacking of the keyboard and women laughing in the background.

"No—it never went into that account. We used it to pay down on your credit line."

"I thought I said pay some on the credit line and put the rest in my account. To use the payment and the amount in my account to convince the board to extend the line. Judas, Carroll—do we need to start writing this stuff down?"

"I probably should have. I must have forgotten what you said after you dropped the check off. I can straighten it out," Carroll said.

"Don't put any in my personal account until I get the IRS to remove the lien. No sense pouring money into that account for them to sit on while they contemplate their navel."

"Where do you want it? You remember RuthAnn moved the transaction account…."

"Hawk hesitated. "Yeah—cripes, I don't know. Can you get it back out of the credit line?"

"Sure, but the board meeting is tomorrow night and I'd like to show some good reduction of that account by then. How much do you need?"

"Need or want?" This was a standard reply from Hawk and Carroll took it in stride.

"Need."

"Fifteen thousand ought to do it."

"I'll have a check for you in thirty minutes."

"Corki will be by and pick it up if that's ok with you. You know Corki…."

"From Miles office? The good looking gal?"

Hawk smiled. "That's her. Put it in a plain white envelope—sealed."

"I'll give it to her...."

"Just the check Carroll—remember you're a married man with a big job in a small community. No hanky panky, don't invite her into your office."

Carroll signed. "What do you do, Hawk, when there are so many of these well built short-skirted young things running around practically asking for a Sugar Daddy...."

"I work. And I'd suggest you do the same."

"Why do I find that hard to believe?" Carroll said.

"Because you are a man of little faith and it is difficult for you to imagine a man like me with soooo much integrity."

"Wow," Carroll said. "It's getting deep in here and the janitors don't come for another four hours. See you later."

"Indeed sir—indeed."

Hawk leaned back in his chair. One friggin more near disaster averted. Is life just a series of disasters a guy tries to miss? Avoid broken bones, get out of military service, don't have a car accident, don't get caught in an occupation where there's a chance someone will hand you your arm after it's been torn off, don't get HIV? It could be looked at that way. Fortunately that's not how I look at it.

The phone rang.

"Hawk Neilson here."

"Hi Hawk."

It took him a second to recognize his ex-wife. "Edith—what a surprise. How are you?"

"I'm fine. Thought you'd be interested to know how well you taught me during the short time we were married about the important things in life."

"Yeah—such as?"

"Such as eavesdropping on an attorney and his client who happened to be close by. Said client happening to be Cruit Johnson and his stated purpose to get a divorce because his wife is living with *our* son."

"I've heard that."

"Well for God's sake, Hawk—check it out. Cruit can be a handful when he gets mad."

"You're Jonathan's mother. You call and tell him to kick her out."

"Get real—he's not going to listen to me."

"Not when you're living with someone yourself."

The line was silent.

"Just thought I'd pass it on," she said. "It could save a funeral where we'd have to be together—God forbid."

"Edith—I have my plate full. I can't run around nursing a thirty-two year old through life. I gave him the best twenty years of my life—so did you. He's on his own, sink or swim."

"Just don't let him get killed, Hawk."

"Cruit's not like that anymore. He seems steady, powerful, and intent on getting his way with persuasion, brilliant arguments, and crafty moves. He's not going to kill anybody."

"I hope you're right. Well—have a good day for me," she said and hung up.

Have a good day for her? Now what the hell does that mean?

4:00 p.m. Wednesday, June 10, 1998

In his home office, Hawk laid out the file on the house trade. He rifled through it confirming what he thought he remembered about it. Looked ok to him. House was rented the requisite amount of time, rent receipts and tax and insurance receipts in order. Corki kept a good file. Now, if the file corresponded with the books she was bringing over, David Bires IRS agent, unrepentant ultra snoop, would be shown the dual records and the IRS filing and the consistency of all three and sent on his merry way.

George Arbuckle didn't ring or knock—just walked in the first floor office and left the door open behind him. He pointed at a bottle of pills on Hawk's desk.

"What are those?"

"Viagra."

"They work?"

"Don't know."

"I thought you were taking some kind of drink for that," George said.

"It was a placebo."

"I'll be damned." He scratched his head then unfolded a map he had brought. "It looks to me like that 640 acres inside Slim's ranch can be reached by an old irrigation ditch right-of-way and if that's so we could scratch out a passable road and get to it. That doesn't increase its value for farming or ranching, but it does make it accessible and somebody besides Slim could use it, much to his consternation." He looked up from the map with a quizzical frown on his forehead and a question in his eyes.

"Where'd you learn such big words, George?" Hawk said.

"What—consternation?"

"No. Accessible."

George smiled. "Every team needs one college graduate on it. I'm going to go check the Irrigation District's old records in the morning. If we end up buying that land to close this thing, I want to make sure we can get to it without knocking on Slim's door every time for permission."

Hawk leaned back in his chair. "So you're not against buying the land?" he said.

George shook his head. "I think we can spare—what— maybe $100,000 out of $24,000,000 to buy it. What if we only get $60,000 for it? So what—big deal. Each of us leaves about $8,000 in the land from our $3,000,000—I can live with that."

"You're forgetting the $1,200,000 we need to pay back for the front end expenses," Hawk said.

George threw a hand into the air. "Even with that, I'd do it in a heart beat."

"Let me know what you find out from the records."

"I will. See you in the morning."

"Yeah. George…" Hawk waved his hand at the open door. "…don't come barging in like that anymore. Try knocking."

George nodded, then looked up. "Why?"

"I might be doing something I don't want you to see," Hawk said.

"Yeah—like what?"

"I haven't decided yet, but when I do you'll be the first to know. Just practice knocking, ok?"

George nodded. "Ok."

There should be a time in a man's life when he enjoys a certain amount of privacy. This swinging door crap has got to stop. Nobody knocks, rings the doorbell, calls first—they just pop through the door like a coyote bringing home a rabbit.

5:15 p.m. Wednesday, June 10, 1998

When Corki arrived she was carrying a pizza so large she couldn't reach all the way around it with her free arm.

"I didn't know they made them that big," Hawk said.

"It's a new super size. You also get two thirty-two ounce drinks. I brought Pepsi for you."

"Put that thing in the oven—if it'll fit—and let's go over these points so I can tell Mr. IRS hello and goodbye in the same sentence."

They sipped on their drinks and went through the sequence of events establishing the purchase of the house, the holding period, when it became a rental, who it was rented to and for how much; found copies of tax returns for the years he had depreciated it, and documented the transaction when he had used it in an exchange for an apartment house.

The second part was verifying that the apartment house had been strictly an investment, that none of his relatives had lived there free, and that he had moved his basis in the house into the apartment house. Everything looked clean.

Somewhere between the second and third slice of pizza, Hawk slipped the lid off the Viagra bottle and tilted one and a half tablets into his hand. He had split several and had to jostle the bottle to get the half pill to come out. They went down alright with the Pepsi. He had counted carefully and from what Doc and the pharmacist had said he should allow twenty to thirty minutes for them to work.

"You go on up and get ready," Hawk said. "I'll finish up here."

He put the left over pizza in the refrigerator, wiped the wet rings off the glass from the drinks and turned out the lights. As a precautionary measure he locked the French doors into his office.

You never know when George might just walk in.

He felt it straining against his slacks and started for the stairs when the phone rang. For an instant he thought about not answering it but reversed course and picked it up.

"Hello," he said softly.

"Hawk?"

"Yeah."

"Barnyard Maynard here—you busy?"

Hawk looked around. "I'll call you back."

"You in the middle of something?"

Silence

"You got something going—really?" Maynard stayed with it.

"Uh huh. I'll call you back."

"You take a blue-boy?" Maynard said, his voice rising.

Hawk coughed slightly. "Yeah."

"Can you overdose on those things?"

"We'll find out."

It was after midnight before he had enough blood in his head to think properly. He looked at Corki, lying on her stomach, long dark hair stretching down her shoulders and wondered if he had anything left for another try. He cuddled her and she moved into him.

"Wow," she said. "That thing has a heart and set of lungs of its own."

Chapter 11

8:45a.m. Thursday, June 11, 1998

Stoddard Greening was doing half spins in his chair, his arms across his chest and a one-third smile on his face when Hawk came into the office.

Hawk spoke first. "Why the Cheshire grin?"

"Slim bought off on the deal."

Hawk exploded. "Stoddard—that's great!

Stoddard's smile widened. "He knew Royal's ground cause he had bid on it when it was sold for taxes a number of years back. Offered to let us elk hunt on it if it closes."

"If it closes? It's damn well gonna close tomorrow at 3:30."

"That's what I told him and..."

"Get the documents to escrow for..."

"...Already did that," Stoddard said.

Hawk stopped. The action had picked up and obviously Stoddard was doing something to get it done. His thinking, his head shaking had turned to action. He was a worthy partner, one who earned respect and laid down a track record in this county. Now—who was left? The Indians and BIA and coming to an agreement with Royal on the value of the high pasture land. Where to start?

9:30 a.m. Thursday, June 10, 1998

Cruit crossed the cinder track, across the grass football field and toward the bleachers where Hawk sat high up near the broadcast booth. Cruit paused at the first step then sprinted up the stairs, his knee action high and straight just like he had done on the gridiron. He passed Hawk, went to the top, turned and came down. He was a little breathless.

"Coach would have made me do it again," Cruit said.

"Not bad for a twenty-five year lay off," Hawk said.

Cruit sat down beside him.

They looked out over the football field, brown spots where the baseball players had worn it down now that their game was having their season on it. It was quiet, peaceful.

"You miss the high school days?" Cruit said.

"No—not any more. I'm here a lot of days anyway, helping out in spring training, but there has been so much change—I'm not connected that much anymore."

"And, of course, I haven't been," Cruit said. He rubbed his hands and looked at the palms. "I had my best days here and no regrets. The regrets started when I found other things to do instead of get through college."

"You had a good scholarship," Hawk said.

"I did—but I squandered that along with a big chunk of my life. Thought I could do anything I wanted to without thinking of others. Don't know where I got that idea, but it sure reigned supreme with me for a while."

"Heard through the grapevine that you filed for divorce?" Hawk said. He wanted it out of the way before they talked about the land.

Cruit looked at him. "Stuff travels fast doesn't it?"

Hawk nodded.

He looked toward the goal posts. "Haven't filed—but I'm ready to. Can't figure out what to do."

"Hope you don't think I had anything to do with Jonathan getting together with your wife?" Hawk said.

"No. I don't know why I expected her to just stay put while I spent a good part of our married life in the pen. It wasn't very bright of me."

"We all do things that aren't very bright. Its called getting experience…"

Cruit chuckled. "I sure got that—in spades."

Hawk swallowed. "On the land trade—I've figured out a way that might make it possible to deed the river frontage—on both sides of the river—to the tribe." He looked Cruit in the eye. "What I need is the tribe's consent to manage the fishery using the same rules Fish & Wildlife would use if they owned it."

"I don't have any idea what those rules are…"

"I know," Hawk said. "But I can't see how managing the fishery that way would be any problem for the tribe—do you?"

Hawk cussed himself. He had asked a question that could be answered with a 'yes' or 'no' letting Cruit out of expounding on the point if he chose not to. Not a very good counseling job.

"Hawk—I just don't know. What do they want done that we would object to?"

"Just look at the fisheries they manage down river from

this piece. The fish are getting through there to get up to this place so they must be doing what's required. The steelhead are just starting to rebound and it has to be from their management practices. If the tribe will agree to that I think I can pull it together."

Cruit hunched his shoulders. "And we give up—what?"

"I guess the commercial land you didn't want more of."

Cruit smiled and turned his face full to Hawk. "Why don't you buy that from us—we need some cash in this deal?"

"This is a land exchange, not a buy out."

"We need some cash," Cruit said.

"Dammit Cruit—there is no cash!" Hawk was amazed at how his voice carried.

"How are you getting paid? You taking land or cash?"

Hawk took a deep breath. "We're here to discuss you getting the river piece with all the ancestral background, the fishing and hunting. So you have to give up something to get it."

"I understand that. But we need some cash. You buy some of the commercial land from us for cash and maybe we can make the deal. You're getting cash aren't you?" Cruit smiled at him as he stood up. "Share a little of your cash with us poor Indians, Hawk. Just think what you can put on that commercial land; gas stations, motel, restaurant, bar…"

"Like we don't have enough of those around here already…" Hawk said.

"Yeah—but these would be *yours*." He handed Hawk his card. "Call me when you know which of our lands you want to buy."

"Cruit—this deal is closing tomorrow at 3:00…"

"Maybe it will and maybe it won't. See you around."

Hawk watched him go down the stairs two at a time and admired his athleticism. He turned the card in his hand.

"Well I'll be damned," he said, and slid the card into his shirt pocket.

10:40 a.m. Thursday, June 11, 1998

"Where you been?" Wev said when Hawk came through the front door. "We've been looking for you."

"Talking with Cruit."

"Will he take the deal?"

"Wants us to buy their commercial land. What do you think that's worth?"

"I have no idea—how much?" Wev said.

"Probably two million," Hawk said. "We're getting drained of our cash pretty damn fast."

"It's not a bad site to develop."

"Like who's going to develop it—you?"

"No—but somebody ought to want it."

"Look—I'm trying to hold enough cash for us in this deal to justify the four years we've put into it. We go buying chunks of land here and there and then we've got taxes and insurance to pay on them, and no cash."

"Tomorrow's coming…" Wev started.

"…My God I know about tomorrow," Hawk exploded. "Start thinking of something that will help on this deal instead of reminding me of the calendar!"

"I was just trying…"

"…Well quit trying and actually do it. We're not practicing now, this is the big leagues. These ex-professional athletes running around town are always looking back at what they were. We've got an opportunity here to make a real differ-ence—now—late in our lives."

Wev spread his hands. "What do you want me to do, Hawk?"

"Call the BIA and see if they have any other problems with this deal if the tribe gets the river property—and don't let them off if they say 'we don't think so.' Get a definite, firm, positive answer from that political appointee."

Hawk used his sore hand to close his office door care-fully. He looked at his watch. It was lunchtime in Washington

DC—poor time to try and reach the Senator. He dialed Carroll at the bank.

"Morning Carroll—did IRS lift that lien yet?"

"We missed you at breakfast," Carroll said.

"What—you couldn't eat without me?"

"We managed. It would have been good to have further instructions in the use of the knife and fork however."

"Yeah, I've been neglectful in that." He waited. "The lien?"

"No. But I was able to put that money on the credit line so they can't get at that."

"Fine—just great. I sell a property at a big discount to get transaction cash and it goes to reduce my debt with you—no big help if the board doesn't renew the credit line tonight."

"They will Hawk. I got a feeling that making that payment will turn them into a real generous bunch."

"Hope you're right Carroll. Let me know when IRS does their duty."

"I'll do it."

11:04 a.m. Thursday, June 11, 1998

The pain started slowly from the outside of his stomach and at first Hawk tried to dismiss it as anxiety. He reassured himself that the deal was coming along as well as could be expected and when he tied up the last three loose ends, it would all come together tomorrow, just like he had planned.

Juggling isn't my strong suit, yet I've got more balls in the air then I can keep track of.

He went to the blackboard again and wiped it clean.

Who needs my final efforts to close and what have I left out of the explanation that would get them to the table. It's very logical, very clean and simple. Each party getting something they want more than what they're giving up. So—why was it being hung up by the....

The phone interrupted his thoughts.

"Hello, Hawk here."

"Frank Cline on this end…"

Hawk could see the office he had helped decorate in Washington D.C. The Idaho spruce wall panels, the Jefferson County record elk head and record white tail deer head one on either side behind the plain cedar desk. He knew Senator Cline would have his tie loosened and his feet on the desk. He was that way in Boise. "Good morning Senator."

"It's afternoon here."

"You're so right. Does it make any difference?" Hawk said.

"Yeah—I'm closer to scotch time than you are."

Hawk laughed. "We've organized your re-election committee, got a good chairman and a small office in one of Royal's buildings. I opened a bank account for the re-election committee with $1,000."

"Is that a loan or a contribution?" the Senator said.

"It's a loan until we close this deal."

"Fair enough. I talked to the head of BIA and he's telling me that the guy in Boise really has authority to approve this deal or kill it. What's his name…?"

"Dan Hogue."

"Yeah—that's him. You had any further discussions with him?"

"My last conversation with him was before my meeting with the tribe and Cruit Johnson. He said then that if the Indians approved it he would go along with it. Couldn't get anything else out of him really."

"Well, that's the side your bread is buttered on. I might have some influence down there but not as much as your locals if he's going to call the shots."

"It shouldn't really need any shot calling, the result is so logical to all of the parties that…"

"You know better than that Hawk. Everything comes from a political motivation, win-lose. I'll put in a call to him if you want me to but my take on it at this point is for you to work it locally. Having a senator call him from Washington isn't going to sway him one way or ..."

"Don't call him yet. I'll get a reading on it and give you a call. You going to be in the office tomorrow?"

"Got a committee meeting until about 10 o'clock but then I should be around. My staff can always find me."

"I may need you sober," Hawk said.

Cline laughed. "I give some of my best advice after 5:00 o'clock and the cocktail hour."

"Yeah—to the other party."

"Hawk—it shames me to count you as a friend. See ya."

The phone went dead.

11:15 a.m. Thursday, June 11, 1998

The intercom buzzed on Royal Cunningham's desk.

"Mr. Neilson to see you."

Royal cleared his desk and stood up to greet Hawk. "Coffee?"

"Sure—cream and sugar please."

Royal's chair was pushed back a foot from the desk. He folded his arms over his chest. Hawk had seen that stance many times. Whether Royal was buying or selling it was the same— his negotiating strategy was to be the one who cared the least about the outcome. Hawk stirred his coffee and wondered how he was going to open the talk.

"That old building you sold me sure needs a bunch of work," Royal said.

"Buildings need that frequently. You gotta love the tenants though, they are so helpful."

Royal smiled. "You didn't come to talk about that."

"No," Hawk said. He sipped his coffee. "This Colombian coffee?"

"Come on, Hawk—I'm a busy man."

"Earlier this week I made you a good deal on the apartments. I need a good deal on your land up in the pass."

"That's very good land. I've got great plans for that piece of ground."

"Come on, Royal. It's the arctic. The polar bears only leave it for two months out of the year and then they can hardly get out for the mud."

"You don't want it, then, do you?"

This wasn't the way he had planned to enter the negotiations. He blew on the coffee and ventured another sip.

"We don't want it," Hawk said. "But we need to buy it for another guy in our deal. He's the one that thinks he can live with the low oxygen content at that altitude."

"I *think* you are asking how much I want for it?" Royal pursed his lips, looked at Hawk and got nonverbal approval to continue. "I have spent some time thinking about that and researched my records since your man came by to inquire about it. Has the potential purchaser seen it?"

"He knows about it."

"Then if you are willing to go ahead, I presume there will be no contingencies in the final agreement?"

Royal sounded so cotton-pickin formal.

"I need a deed by tomorrow afternoon," Hawk said.

Royal put his elbows on the desk and frowned. "Why are you always so short of time?"

"My life moves in short cycles. How much do you think it's worth?"

"One million dollars."

Hawk's coffee hand froze halfway to his mouth. There it was. The opening bid in the Buy-something-from-Cunningham auction.

"For crying-out-loud—you bought that land at tax sale for a lousy $150,000."

"Don't call $150,000 lousy. I was the high bidder and that was several years ago."

"Yeah, and since then the cattle market has gone to hell,

the town hasn't grown, no new industry is planned forty miles out of town and above the clouds, and you think it has gone up to $1,000,000."

"Was that a question or a statement?" Royal said.

"Take it for what you want."

"To close tomorrow and give you a deed, I need a sizeable non-refundable earnest money—say $25,000 and a provision that if you don't pay for it tomorrow the price goes up $5,000 a week until it closes."

Hawk rubbed his chin. "Let's work on the price first. I'm thinking $350,000."

Royal unlocked his arms and moved his chair to the desk. "Enjoy the rest of your coffee. It's not Colombian; it's Brazilian fine grind. I wish you luck in your deal."

Wow—we're there already. The goodbye; the no deal sign off.

"What's the best price you can give me today?" Hawk said.

"You may have all day to drink coffee and dicker with me on this property but I have many important things to do."

"What's the best price?"

"You through with your coffee?"

Hawk put his palm flat on the desk. "Best price—today—cash?"

Royal stared out the window for a full minute. "$500,000—no more dickering."

Hawk put the cup on the desk. "Done."

They stood and shook hands.

"Needs those two provisions I mentioned or no deal," Royal said.

"Understood," Hawk said as he closed the door.

He waited until he was halfway down the back stairs before he smiled. By the time he hit the parking lot he was whistling the theme from The Magnificent Seven.

12:10 a.m. Thursday, June 11, 1998

"You're not eating much, Hawk. You feeling alright?" the waitress said.

"I shouldn't have ordered the chili. I know damn good and well what you make it out of," Hawk said.

"You didn't find any ground glass in it did you?"

"Is that what's hurting my stomach?"

"Could be. We tried everything else."

Stoddard Greening stood in the door looking around the restaurant.

Ella looked at him. "Close the door, Stoddard—you're letting flies in."

"Might help the food some," Stoddard said. "Hawk in here?"

Ella nodded towards the back of the restaurant and Stoddard wandered down the isle chatting with some of the customers. He slid in the booth across the table from Hawk.

"What'd Royal say?" Stoddard said.

"He said $600,000—take it or leave it."

Stoddard was silent for a moment. "Well—I can live with that."

Hawk gave it several seconds. "Actually—I got it for $500,000."

The grin started slowly then spread across his face. "That's pretty good Hawk."

"Not bad for a country boy."

"We're gonna end up buying three places aren't we?" Stoddard said.

"Looks that way."

"How much do you think we'll each have left in cash?"

"Enough."

"Yeah—probably. I mean—you divide up $24 million and we still have a big pot left over don't we? Even if we shell out $2 million for those land parcels."

"Cruit's asking $2 million for the tribe's commercial

land along the highway. It'll be something more than $2 million when it's over. Most likely closer to $3.8 million total, including our up front expenses."

"Even at that we'd end up with something like $3 million apiece, plus a piece of the land parcels." He had his elbows on the table, his face smiling at Hawk. "Hot damn—that'll do it. That'll simply do it."

His smile disappeared and he looked in Hawk's eyes. "You all right, Hawk?"

"You're the second person's asked me that today."

"You look poorly."

"It's the glass they put in this chili, it's shredding my guts."

Chapter 12

1:38 p.m. Thursday, June 11, 1998

After lunch, Hawk and Stoddard found Wev and Ruth-Ann in conference.

"Wev, RuthAnn, can you get the papers for the Nez Perce drawn up? Stoddard will give you the particulars. I need to get Cruit to sign them before he does another dance and changes the deal.

"Does he have the power to sign them?" Wev asked.

"Dammed if I know. Why don't you call the chief and see if he has. If they've given him that power we need to see some sort of tribal resolution signed by the elected members.

I'm not going to escrow tomorrow with something signed by him that's not worth the paper it's written on."

Stoddard and RuthAnn took the files and huddled in the corner office.

He can get along with her better than I can right now.

Hawk called the escrow.

"Good afternoon, Elda. This is Hawkins Neilson. Will you give me a very close estimate of how much money we're gonna need to close our escrow tomorrow."

"Hello, Mr. Neilson. I'm working on that now, give me just a second." He could hear fast fingering on the calculator then Elda said, "You're gonna need $152,347.87 to close, not counting the money going to Royal for his land and to the tribe for their land."

"Would you pass that by Corki at our accountant's office? I'd like her to wave her wand over it and check the figures?"

"Sure," the lady said. "I'll get it over there in twenty minutes."

"Great. Thanks."

Hawk dialed Corki's direct line.

Her sweet voice said, "Hello, Hawk."

"When did you get caller ID?"

"Last month. I gotta know how to answer calls that come in on my personal line." She hit 'personal' pretty hard.

Hawk chuckled. "The escrow is going to fax over the closing statement to you. Go through it with a fine toothed comb and let me know if there are any problems."

Her business voice came back on. "Sure. When do you need it?"

"Like ten minutes after you get it."

"Wow!"

"What's that accounting degree good for if it isn't speedy?"

"Can I blink three times while I'm doing it?"

"If you're fast about it. I need to rake up the closing

money and I don't want to do it twice. Don't have time for mistakes."

"Ok. I'll call you. Do you want me to run it over personally—like to your house?" It was her little girl voice now, not quite pleading but letting it be soft, slow, and girlish.

"No time for that today. But I'll keep it in mind for Saturday."

"Can't Saturday—my boyfriend's coming to town this weekend."

Hawk thought a moment, then decided he could say it. "He worried about you playing around?"

"He doesn't much care about the sexual part of our relationship. He's a nice, caring, comfortable guy to be around—and I like him a lot."

"Is he gay?"

Corki exploded. "Oh for crying-out-loud, Hawk—of course he's not gay. He just doesn't get all that excited about sex."

"You going to marry him?"

"I don't know. If you don't ask me, I might have to marry him. I could do a lot worse."

"Yes you could. And I'm too old and crazy for you…"

"You are not, Hawk. You're great…" She let it taper off, the child-like tone sliding into silence.

"Well, don't let the word out. Let me know when you get the figures."

"I will. Love you."

Hawk hung up the phone without making a commitment. He slumped in his chair, head in his hands. Sue Diggs knocked on the glass and he motioned her to come in.

How long have we been together? Ten—fifteen years? Since my divorce—what's that been? His head was spinning but he managed a smile.

"Hi," he said.

"Hi yourself."

"What're you doing?"

"Wondering if there is anything I can do to help you get the transaction closed." Her long dark hair looked like it had been selectively placed over her shoulders.

"Yeah—loan me $150,000. I'll have it back to you tomorrow by 5:00 p.m."

"No you won't," Sue said. "The checks won't clear until Monday after the recording."

"You're right." Hawk looked up at her. "You've got $150,000 to loan?"

"I can write you a check."

Hawk nodded. An old saw between them. It didn't mean anything. So much didn't mean anything, yet so much did. It was the comfortableness he felt that was important and the knowing what was behind her beauty. The doggedness, the grit to get what she needed for herself and her family. It was an inspiring image for him and he coveted it.

"You feeling alright?" Sue said.

"My God—I need a mirror. What is there about me that people think I'm dying today?"

Sue lifted her palm up. "I didn't say you looked dead. Just that…"

"Just what?" Hawk said.

"Just—you look used up."

"Used up? Hummm." He ran his hand through his hair. "Ok—you can go see Brad at Fish and Game and see if he's gotten approval for the tribe to manage the river under the same rules and regulations F&G uses. He was going to get back to me on it but I haven't heard from him. He would probably respond better to you."

"Yeah—he likes me."

"He likes all girls."

She lifted one eyebrow. "Nothing wrong with that."

"Just check with him will you? My stomach has been hurting for two days and now my head's crashing. I'm not as good as I need to be right now."

"I'll go change into my short skirt," Sue said.

Hawk snorted. "You'll earn your share on this trip."

3:00 p.m. Thursday, June 11, 1998

"RuthAnn—we need to talk," Hawk said.

She came in his office, closed the door and sat properly, knees together in front of his desk barely glancing at the animal heads on the wall, feeling the air tight and stuffy, the air circulation system falling short of meeting the needs of his interior office.

Hawk looked at her. "Escrow says we need $152,347.87—call it $152,500. I had about $120,000 in the transaction account and I put another $75,000, minus $15,000 for personal, from my sale to Royal, against the credit line. You need to draw a check for the $120,000 and I'll put up the balance from the credit line to close it."

"Why can't I take it over there tomorrow when it closes?" she said.

"I don't want to take any chances. You're the only signer on that account and you could get sick, have an accident—anything."

RuthAnn crossed her legs. "I'd feel a lot more comfortable knowing the escrow papers are correct…"

"…Corki's going over them now," Hawk said.

"…**Then** writing the check to the escrow," she finished.

"You can write the check to escrow but I want it today—now. I'll add my check and we'll have it done. No slipups. No last minute wondering."

She sat perfectly still. Hawk looked her right in the eyes and didn't say a word. Both were silent. It was the first time Hawk had ever heard traffic noise in his office or the screen door banging on the restaurant across the back lot.

"Ok," she said and got up to get the checkbook.

Hawk put the company check and his check in an envelope and locked them in his desk.

RuthAnn got up to leave.

He forced himself. "Thank you, RuthAnn."

She looked at him unsmiling. "You're welcome."

3:15 p.m. Thursday, June 11, 1998

Wev put his head in the door. "Can I come in?"

"Sure," Hawk said.

"The Chief said the council had agreed that Cruit could sign up to a point. They need to have full council approval before it closes. They want to know when they can see the papers." Wev said.

"Tell them tomorrow morning. I need them approved by noon and something authorizing Cruit to sign—if he is going to sign for them."

"Yeah—I know." Wev leaned against the wall with his hands in his pockets. "Hawk—I've got a funny feeling about this deal."

"Lose it!"

"It's not that easy."

"Work on it!"

My God…how many hundreds of times has Wev considered failure an option? He's looking for all the world like a whipped puppy. Our Granddad's backbone is absent in his makeup and there's not a damn thing I can do about it for the rest of his life.

"Hawk, it's just that…"

"Wev—there is not time to diagram feelings of doom here. Get me the papers, I'll take them to Cruit, and we'll button this thing up tomorrow."

"Yeah, but what about Fish and …"

"Sue is out getting Fish and Game to sign off as we speak," Hawk said.

"…And Slim…"

"…Slim's agreed to take Royal's high ground."

"Oh…"

"Wev—we're closing tomorrow. Get me the Indian papers," he pleaded. "Please."

Wev shouldered himself off the wall and walked out. He was back in five minutes with a large white envelope. It was addressed to the Nez Perce Tribe. In the upper left hand corner was the bronze return address sticker of Pine Ridge Properties LLC, their new company for this transaction.

"Looks kinda good doesn't it?" Wev said.

Hawk nodded. "Where do you think I can find Cruit this time of day?"

Wev took in a deep breath. "He could be down at Jonathan's trailer."

"You act like you've seen him?"

Wev nodded. "Just a bit ago."

Hawk wondered about calling Jonathan's number then thought better of it. He didn't want to tie this signing into the messy divorce that could be coming.

"Could you keep an eye on him and let me know when he leaves so I can get to him with these papers?" Hawk said.

Wev perked up. "I'll do it."

3:47 p.m. Thursday, June 11, 1998

"Hawk, this is Carroll. The Board just took a recess and I wanted to call you about two things."

"After you went to the bathroom?"

"No—before. Listen—they're having a real tough debate about renewing your line. They think you're using it like a permanent loan and aren't making meaningful reductions on it until crunch time when you need to re-borrow it again."

"So…?"

"Right now the verbal vote is to call the balance due and not allow any further borrowing until we get all new information on you and the new company you're working under."

"Carroll—I just wrote a $35,000 check on that account assuming the line would be extended, like we discussed. That check is to cover our closing costs—along with the $120,000 from the transaction account RuthAnn moved out of your bank. That check has to clear."

"Hawk—I don't know what I can tell them that will change the present vote."

"Tell them anything you have to tell them, but get it cleared. For hell's sake, by Monday I'll be worrying how you're going to get FDIC insurance to cover my personal $13 million deposit."

"They're not as sure of that deal as you are."

Hawk pressed the palm of his hand against his forehead. "Remind them that it was me who brought that bank into town. It was me who asked them to be on the board, and me who put the first hundred thousand capital into it. And it was me that hired you to run it."

Carroll replied in a matter-of-fact manner. "If you re-call, you took that hundred grand out the next week."

"That's true—but I got it started and it's been going ever since."

"I know—I know."

"Well—call me back with their approval. Or—just let it ride as it is until Monday—then we'll all know. That's it!" Hawk pounded his fist on his desk. "Just leave the credit line alone until Monday, then they can call it or extend it, whatever. Can you do that?"

"I'll try. They're going back in, I gotta git."

"I'm counting on you, Carroll. Don't fail me," Hawk said to a dead line.

4:10 p.m. Thursday, June 11, 1998

Wev called and said Cruit had gone to the Veterans Club. Hawk drove down there and found him with a group of tribal leaders playing pool. He walked in and stayed in the shadows as Cruit lined up the cue ball, the strange bitter smell of old beer, smoke and carpet that hadn't been cleaned in years pushed its way into his nose. When Cruit missed the shot, Hawk waved the envelope at him and motioned him over to a table in the back corner.

"What kind of a signal is that?" Cruit said.

"White man's signal. Means I've got something for you; come here...please."

"I like that please."

"I'm always polite to the younger generation," Hawk said.

"By only three years."

"Well—what measure do you want to use?"

"Hawk—you'd argue with a possum if he'd answer back."

"I've had them answer back—lots of times."

Cruit chuckled. "What have you got?"

The closing papers for tomorrow. I want you to take them and go over them with your trained legal eyes and then get them ready to sign tomorrow. If you are going to sign for the tribe..."

"...I'm not."

Hawk cocked his head and looked at him. "Who is?"

"We haven't decided yet." Cruit slid the papers out of the envelope.

Hawk smelled a rat. "Get a tribal authorization for the signer and have him at the escrow at 3:00 tomorrow, assuming these papers are alright with you. If you see anything you don't like, let me know right away. I'll be available on my cell phone."

Cruit shoved the papers back in the envelope. "You're buying the commercial land on the highway?"

Hawk nodded.

"Paying $2 million like we talked?"

Hawk nodded.

Cruit pushed back his chair. "I'll see what I can do."

Hawk nodded again and bit his lip until he felt the pain.

"By the way, Hawk. You don't look too good. You alright?"

"Never felt better."

Cruit cocked his head, his eyes squinted. "Ok."

Hawk sat in the chair for a couple of minutes and breathed deeply trying to ease the pain in his stomach. When he bent over to get in his car it hurt again.

4:31 p.m. Thursday, June 11, 1998

Hawk slowed down to the speed limit, flipped open his cell phone and dialed the bank.

"Is Carroll there, Peggy?"

"Hi, Hawk. He's just coming out of the boardroom. Let me see if I can get him for you."

"Thanks."

"He's going to his office. He'll be with you in a minute."

"Thank you, Peggy."

Hawk pictured the lanky Carroll walking along the carpeted big open space in front of the teller line, smiling at the young tellers, letting them see the man who ran the bank, continued their employment and signed their checks.

Carroll picked up the line. "Hello, Hawk."

"How'd it go?"

"Not good. IRS didn't remove the levy on your account and the board felt it would be bad judgment to continue your line until you get it cleared up—so they're calling it due now."

Hawk's head pounded; his guts boiled. He pulled over to the side of the road, opened the car door and threw up. The door-ajar chime rang like Big Ben while he emptied himself of lunch. He shuddered and reached for his handkerchief.

He could hear Carroll on the phone. "Hawk—you ok? Hawk?"

He pushed the off button and dropped it on the passenger seat. When he had mopped his face and mouth he threw the handkerchief off the road and took a couple deep breaths. His stomach only hurt when he bent forward. Maybe he could stay more erect. He eased the car into gear and headed toward the house, his head pushed back against the head rest.

6:32 p.m. Thursday, June 11, 1998

　　　When Hawk stumbled into the house the phone was ringing. He picked it up and heard Sue's voice.
　　　"Can I charge our bar bill to your account?" she asked.
　　　"You and who else?" he growled.
　　　"Brad. He's gone to the restroom and I don't have any money with me."
　　　"You never do."
　　　"I count on you to have it."
　　　"That's why you're so damned expensive."
　　　"Here he comes…" she whispered.
　　　"Ok. But remember—you're my girl friend not his."
　　　"Oh, Hawk, you're so sweet. Bye."
　　　His stomach finally stopped hurting. He just needed a good evacuation to get his natural zing back. The scotch bottle was half full and he poured it straight, then thinking of his stomach he added a dash of water.
　　　It was that time of day when the sun was down but it wasn't dark yet. The western mountains truly looked purple, which always reminded him of the phrase 'purple mountain majesty' in the song "America the Beautiful." When they were growing up they always laughed at that because everyone knew the mountains weren't purple.
　　　From the lawn chair he watched the river and wondered if the mosquitoes would be bad when they came out of the grass and trees. The sound of a flute came to his ears, proud, strong notes that moved back and forth between mournful and honest claims of strength. He had never heard it before but it had to come from across the river. Too dark to see who was there— besides it was a public park—it could be anybody.

But why would a flute play on this night?

He drank his scotch and listened to the pleasant sound. When he was through with his drink the flute sounds were still drifting across the water and there had been no repetition.

Who would know that many sounds and songs? Plenty had the time to do it, but who had the time and the talent?

While he was engrossed in the music the phone rang. It was Slim.

"I came in tonight so the Mrs. and I could go close this escrow tomorrow. We still going there at 3:00 our time?"

"That's right, Slim. How was haying?"

"Hot, dusty, hard—lots of rattlesnakes this year. I'll bet we caught a dozen of them in the bailer."

"You charge extra for hay with a rattlesnake in the bale?"

"Only if the head is worth mounting."

"Save me one for a hat band," Hawk said.

"I'll do that. And I'll call you when we're through signing down here."

"Ok. Call me if you run into any problems at closing."

"You better believe it. Bye."

The flute had stopped and the stars were coming out in the eastern half of the night sky. He debated about having another scotch but let it go. Cruit might call; Corki was going to report on the escrow figures; and Sue, bless her little larcenous heart, was waltzing Brad around and would bring back the final report on F&G.

There was nothing he could do now. It was in motion, and like a large ship underway, it just needed a slight directional adjustment from time to time. He went in and put three frozen seafood kabobs in the oven, peeled a carrot, and poured an ice tea.

The check. The one for $35,000 that he had written on his credit line. It was no good. Would escrow think to verify those funds before they closed? If they didn't he would have plenty of money after the closing to clear it. They knew him well enough to skip the verification, but the state laws had gotten tougher on escrows to make sure they closed with certified funds. He needed a backup.

He dialed Royal's number from memory.

"Cunningham's…"

"Hi, Royal. Hawk here—you asleep?"

"While I am up early enough to get the worm, I don't retire at seven. What's on your mind—you backing out of our land deal?"

"No. I need to ask a favor. I wrote a substantial check that I can't cover until Monday afternoon. I may need to verify funds on it. If I absolutely have to have it, would you loan me $35,000 until Monday?"

"You know my hard money loan terms?"

"Of course." He could virtually hear Royal's mind working.

"Since there won't be any time to build up interest on it, why don't we just say five points?"

"If I need the loan," Hawk said.

"Of course. If you need it—five points. What's the security?"

"My word."

"Hawk—we've discussed this before. I can't foreclose on your word."

"You've got $25,000 earnest money on your land from me, why…"

"Hawk, that is a non-refundable earnest money to secure purchase of the land, not a bargaining chip."

"My house then."

"Your house?" He was silent a moment. "How much do you owe on it?"

"Around $200,000."

"That could work. Five points and a second on your house."

"A third," Hawk said. "I've got a second on it—part of the $200,000."

"Ok. Done. I'll make out a check and leave it in my top drawer in case you need it and I'm not around. Ask Renee to get it for you."

"Thank you, Royal. You are a friend in need."

"It's the least I can do. Now you can have another scotch."

"How did you know?"

Royal chuckled. "It took one to get up the nerve to call and now that you have what you want you can relax with the second."

"Think I will. Good night, Royal."

Hawk reached for the bottle. He held it a minute in both hands thinking of what Royal had just said. What he had deduced from them knowing each other for so long and understanding how they worked as a benefit to each other.

It is an interesting relationship. I wonder how long it has been going on without me thinking about it? He uncorked the bottle and poured an ounce. Well—that hole is plugged. He lifted the glass.

Chapter 13

9:17 p.m. Thursday, June 11, 1998

The headlights flashed across his bedroom ceiling. Hawk closed his book and listened. First the door, then the steps. He knew those steps and he smiled as he put the book on the nightstand and turned out the light.

"Move over," Sue said.

"I am over. I was reading on my side of the bed."

"Brad danced so close he made my nipples sore and it was either him or you."

"I'm sure he is disappointed."

Sue slipped into bed. "I left him with a competent gal at the Longhorn. You feeling better?"

"I am now. Oh—your hands are cold. And your feet!"

"Oh shut up, you big baby." She moved down on him. "Is that better?"

"Much."

They lay together, arms and legs entwined, heads close. Hawk's mind was running over the day's events. "Did Brad get Fish & Game approval of the deal?"

"Umhuh."

"He won't back out now that you've left him in the lurch?"

"I told you I left him in competent hands. Besides—I've got the papers in my purse."

Hawk smiled. "What a gal."

"I'm worth it, huh?" She put her head on his shoulder.

"You're still the most expensive."

"Yah—but I'm worth it, huh?"

"Quit tickling."

"I'm worth it aren't I? Just say yes and I'll quit."

"Yes—dammit, you're worth it."

"Ok."

10:30 p.m. Thursday, June 11, 1998

Hawk's cell phone was ringing from his pants pocket. He got out of bed and found it.

"Hawk—this is Cruit. You awake?"

"Sure—what is it?"

"Just one thing. I see in these papers that you are acting as a principal and you say that you are reselling the land to undisclosed parties for a potential profit. That so?" Cruit said.

"Yes." Hawk felt the back of his neck getting warm.

"Can you tell me who you're selling it to—and for how much?"

"That's why it says 'undisclosed parties'."

"Yeah, I know. But what if it's worth more than you are paying us for it?"

"What if the river property you're getting is worth more than what you're giving?" Hawk said. His throat constricted.

"Hard to value land used for conservation and a fishery…"

"…And a burial ground," Hawk inserted.

"…And a burial ground. Our commercial land has comparable sales all over the valley," Cruit said.

"Cruit—you brought up the sale of your land to us and priced it at $2,000,000. We agreed to buy it to facilitate this transaction. There are other properties we could buy for that $2 million that already have a motel, gas station, and bar on them, as you suggested."

"How much you selling the land for?"

"We don't have a buyer for it. It just came up this week when you and I talked at the stadium."

"Then why is the profit paragraph in there?" Cruit persisted.

"Come on Cruit—you know the answer to that. It's to keep the seller from coming back on us if, and I repeat **if,** we make a profit selling it later on."

"Ok. I can report to the council that you do not have a planned sale of the commercial land at this time and you don't know what it is worth to a potential buyer?"

"Correct," Hawk said. He felt Sue's hand on his neck as she moved it over the tense muscles.

Cruit coughed slightly. "Council meeting is at dawn tomorrow. I'll call you after that."

"Just remember to tell them that they asked for and got, the hunting, fishing, and management rights and the burial grounds—all important tribal goals—all solved with this transaction. And don't forget the authorization for whoever is going to sign for the tribe."

"Night, Hawk."

He pulled the phone away from his ear and looked at it like it had a life of its own. "Dammit—he hangs up without answering my questions."

"That last thing you said was a statement—not a question," Sue said.

"Oh—right—so it was."

"Come back to bed and I'll give you a massage."

Hawk flicked the covers over. "How much is that?"

"They charge fifty-five dollars in Boise," Sue said.

"We're not in Boise."

"Well, counting transportation from Boise, food and lodging, hair and nails, and time to and from on the road, I'd say $350."

"That sounds about how you price your services."

"Shut up and relax. You need to be sharp tomorrow."

Hawk closed his eyes and felt the deep satisfaction of the massage. The next thing he knew the sun was coming up over the hill and it was Friday morning.

5:55 a.m. Friday, June 12, 1998

He lay on his back listening to the mockingbirds chattering and the occasional raven caw. Early morning had always been a special time of day for him. This morning it heralded the mightiest financial effort of his life. He took a deep breath and thought about the debts he had listed and mentally paid off with his share of the proceeds. At least twenty-five times he had figured to the dollar what he would have left after closing, minus the transaction costs and his personal debts.

The residue was now a problem. Not only his sons but also his ex-wife, his mother-in-law, the IRS and Sue would have their hands out. It's hard in a small community to avoid the information zipping around town.

Hawk just closed a big deal—paid off all his debts. Won't have to do another thing the rest of his life if he doesn't want to. Royal says Hawk paid him in gold! All kinds of stuff.

Well—I won't tell anybody anything—just let them wonder.

He felt that Sue was gone. He listened for her breathing but there was nothing. Yet he was reluctant to open his eyes and confirm anything. Finally he rolled over and trundled to the shower. The alarm went off when he got to the bathroom and he let it buzz.

He showered, dressed and laid out his vitamins on the counter. One by one he swallowed them with spicy V8 juice while he rubbed in the Rogaine. He looked in the mirror. The Rogaine didn't seem to be making much progress, but it did make it easier to comb.

The sun was up when he opened the restaurant door. "Morning, Ella."

"Good morning, Hawk. You look rested."

"Finally had a good nights sleep. Everyone been telling me I looked like warmed over pizza and I took it to heart. Had a scotch and slept like a baby."

"More'n likely you slept with a babe," Ella said.

"Ella—and you a church going woman…"

"Church people know about that sort of thing too."

Carroll and Thaddeus walked in together, each reading a newspaper as they passed through the door and down the aisle.

"The Mariners lost again. I don't know why they don't spend some decent money on a pitcher," Carroll said.

"Why don't you lend it to them?" Thaddeus said.

"Better yet—quit betting on them," Hawk said.

Both of them looked at Hawk and held up their coffee cups. In unison they recited:

"This is the day you close your deal.
You need to stay on an even keel.
Drink only coffee and smell only flowers
So you can enjoy the ivory towers."

They both drank.

"That's the worst rhyme I've ever heard," Hawk said.

"It came from the heart," Thaddeus said. "Took us two hours."

"The two professions where hearts are not required—banking and law," Hawk said.

"Wow—he's touchy today," Ella said as she filled their cups.

They ordered, drank coffee and read the newspaper with an occasional hello to locals they new. After they had eaten and stacked the dishes—something that Ella hated—the day's work began.

"I've not scheduled any clients today so I'll be available if you need me," Thaddeus said.

"Thanks. I don't know if we will or not, but you never know what little changes might be required at closing." Hawk looked at Carroll. "I wrote that check anyway. If escrow calls to verify funds, can you cover for me?"

Carroll shook his head. "Haven't thought about it. I guess I could say it's good if the deal closes. That's when they'll need it. If it doesn't close they don't care if it's good or not—do they?"

"Will you tell them it's good? It's plain logic. If you honor the check and they close, then I have the funds to make it good. If it doesn't close, it doesn't make any difference if the check is good or not."

"Thaddeus," Carroll said. "Am I breaking any law by saying that to the escrow?"

"Chapter 12, paragraph 7 of the Penal Code of the State of Idaho. Thou shalt not lie to an escrow officer seeking pertinent information from a responsible official of any lending institution."

"That let's Carroll out—he's no responsible official," Hawk said.

"No—I don't know of any, Carroll," Thaddeus said. "Of course, it's a lie in the face of the evidence, but no one will be hurt by it either way. Hawk's right. They don't need the money unless it closes; if it closes there is money. Seems pretty cut and dried to me. Course a judge might see it differently—say about seven years at hard labor."

"Oh good. I was needing a vacation," Carroll said. "You are going to pay off the line when this closes aren't you Hawk?"

"I'm going to pay off everything."

"My God—what a feeling that will be, huh?" Thaddeus said.

Hawk rested his head on his hands. "Stuns me to think about it," He said.

"It should happen to all of us when we're you're age," Carroll said. "Just think—single, not only debt free but stinking wealthy…"

"Don't call wealth stinking."

"Right," Thaddeus said. "You may address it as obscene."

"Not obscene either," Hawk said. "You guys have never had this kind of risk. You wouldn't know how to handle it. It takes brains, brawn, and guts. You both get paid for every hour you work, whether you produce anything or not."

"That's pretty harsh," Carroll said.

"When's the last time you *didn't* get paid for working a forty hour week?" Hawk said.

"Well I haven't…"

"That's the crux of the matter right there. He who takes the risk reaps the reward," Hawk said.

Thaddeus and Carroll looked at each other.

"Well—that takes the cake. We're outta here," Thaddeus said and he tipped up the last of his coffee.

Somehow Hawk had not finished his breakfast, small as it was. He lingered over the paper, the second half of a muffin and coffee. He pulled a clean napkin out of the holder and wrote everything that needed finishing on it. Satisfied, he threw some change on the table, signed the breakfast check with his name and CREDIT on it, and walked out the side door.

7:03 a.m. Friday, June 12, 1998

There was a message on his phone from Cruit. He
returned it. There was no answer. He called Cruit's house, then
the Vet's Club. He didn't know where else to call. He looked
out his window and saw Cruit standing in front of his office,
white envelope in hand, beckoning him. Hawk smiled.
Using my tactics against me.
"Here's your precious papers," Cruit said.
"Any changes?"
In a soft voice looking straight in Hawk's eyes, he said,
"just one."
"Which is?"
"Take a ride with me Hawk. I want to show you some-
thing."
"I've got a thousand things to…"
"I know. This won't take ten minutes," Cruit said.
"Can't you just tell me?"
"Come on, we'll be back by the time we'd be through
arguing."

Two miles out of town was the beginning of the reservation then the highway made a turn to conform to the hillside.
That left a large eyeball shaped parcel of land between the
highway and the river. It was flat, had good visibility from both
directions, and the county zoning commission had allowed it
to be zoned for commercial uses. The tribe had traded for it in
1987 and it had sat vacant since then. It was this land that the
tribe was selling to Hawk. Cruit stopped the car smack-dab in
the middle of it and shut off the engine.
"This is the piece," Cruit said.
"Right," Hawk said.
"The one change?" Cruit said. "The price. He looked
out the car window then turned toward Hawk. "The council
wants $3 million."
Inside Hawk erupted. Not since he had exploded at his

ex-wife's attorney had he felt so incensed. He rolled down the window, looked at the river, felt his heart tear itself into little pieccs with each beat; his guts tightened. He could feel Cruit struggling to remain silent and wondered if it was in him to do so. Involuntarily he nodded his head, swallowed several times, then took a deep breath.

"Are the papers signed?" Hawk said while he looked at the river. He worked at keeping his voice calm.

"Yes."

"That the only change?"

"Yes."

He spun and yelled at Cruit. "Why?"

"I checked recent sales, talked to appraisers and the county assessor. Everyone feels $2 million is low—the council agreed on $3 million"

"What the living hell does the council know about the value of a vacant piece of land in a shrinking county that hasn't attracted a buyer for the last eleven years?" Hawk bellowed.

"Traffic count's over 6,000 vehicles per day," Cruit said.

"Big deal!" Hawk spit out the window.

"Easy for trucks to pull in and out. Halfway between Rapid City and Johnsville—good for tourists, fishermen. You could put a marina on the river, rent boats, sell bait..."

"Yeah—when did you last see one of those guys going to the bank?" Hawk said.

"You'll make it go."

"I'm not going to make it go. It's not going anywhere." Hawk got out of the car and slammed the door. He kicked a rock with the toe of his boot that rose into the air like a football and sailed over the bank into the river.

"That would have been good for two points—just on distance," Cruit said.

"You're bleeding us dry!" Hawk screamed.

"*I'm* not!" Cruit lowered his head and evened the tone of his voice. "It's the council's request. One small change..."

"Judas Priest, Cruit—you think I don't know who is behind their thinking and decision making? I didn't just get off a load of pumpkins!" He picked up a rock and threw it out of sight into the river.

Cruit stood, arms crossed. After a minute of silence, Cruit said, "You about through, Hawk?"

Hawk faced the breeze from the river letting it blow through his hair.

"When I followed you through the line," Cruit started. "The big linebackers had to hit you first before they got a shot at me. You always got up smiling. I looked up to you—still do. You know how to turn lemons into lemonade. The tribe needs the money and if this is their only marketable piece of property, then we gotta sell it—sell it in this deal cause we're not going to find another buyer right soon. You can put $3 million in this just as easy as two—develop it and get back six. You've got those skills. We don't. It'll sit here vacant for another ten years if you don't close this deal."

The math was not hard to do. Hawk divided $1 million by four. Each of them would give up—make that 'invest'— $250,000 more in the land. They would have to live with it. How to present it to the others was causing him a massive headache, but present it he would—what other choice did he have?

7:45 a.m. Friday, June 12, 1998

Cruit dropped him off at the office.

"That took longer than ten minutes?" Hawk said.

Cruit shrugged. "What do I know about business discussions?"

"Get a watch," Hawk snarled.

"Not important to me."

"I can see that." Hawk crawled out of the car. "I'll call you—you got your cell phone?"

Cruit patted his pocket.

"Leave it on so I can reach you this time. And don't hang up on me again." He slammed the car door and Cruit peeled rubber for ten yards across the parking lot.

Hawk opened the office door. He went over to the blackboard in the conference room, picked up the chalk and wrote in large script.

I was the first one in the office AGAIN today.
7:45AM Friday, June 12, 1998.   Hawkins Neilsen

The chalk broke in his hand. He looked glum-faced at the piece in his hand then drew back and threw the stub across the room at the waste basket. It hit the wall and shattered.

Chapter 14

8:00 a.m. Friday, June 12, 1998

No one person knew it all, so they gathered in the conference room sipping their coffee, shuffling their feet and scoot-
ing their chairs. They talked about the game, the weather, and
anything except the transaction.

From the front of the table, Hawk viewed them. George
Arbuckle stood by the coffee machine, having picked his spot
at the table by laying down a legal pad, two pens, and a cup
coaster. RuthAnn led Wev through the doorway and plopped a
large folder on the table between two chairs which she claimed

for herself and Wev. Stoddard Greening looked disheveled and distant as he stirred cream into his decaf.

"Everyone's here," Hawk said taking a deep breath. "Let's get started. Grab a seat, Stoddard before you fall down. I'm passing around a card I want all of you to read—carefully." He pulled Cruit's card out of his pocket. George put on his glasses, read it in silence, smiled, and passed it to RuthAnn. When it got to Stoddard he frowned.

"What does it mean?" he asked.

"Means what it says," Hawk said. "Cruit Johnson— First American Rights Consultant."

"So…"

"So Cruit is a tribe member, almost a lawyer, and now a consultant nation wide for American Indians in any situation. He took me out on the land they want to sell to us. Originally we had agreed on $2 million. After a dawn council meeting they have signed the closing papers—with one change."

Stoddard quit stirring his decaf. Everyone looked at Hawk.

"The price is $3 million."

Eyes were the only things that moved. Everyone did mental calculations of cash they would not get and balanced it against the four years they had spent on this deal.

"Why…"

"It doesn't matter why, Stoddard. We don't have time to delve into further negotiations. We either take it or tell the Indians they're out and see if we can keep the other parts in the exchange. That will mean starting over on many of the transactions we've already cemented. Then we'll have to balance the equities somehow," Hawk said.

"How?" George said.

"I don't know—but paying $3 million for the Indian land is our only alternative to letting it go out the window today. Our time frame is gone. If the Indians pull out because we don't buy their land we'd need new authorizations from all the agencies and the 130 private owners who are geared up to change their property lines tomorrow," Hawk said.

"I knew it would come down to something like this," Wev said. "Just as we get to the end of our rope…"

"Hold the expressions of gloom," Hawk said. "I don't like sinking another million dollars in that ground any more than you do. It's been vacant for ever. But my credit line is due at the bank. All the money we borrowed to get this deal to this point is due Monday and dammit, I hate to say it, but I'd rather have a million less profit than let the deal die on this one point."

There was not a sound in the room.

Stoddard licked his stirring stick and crossed his legs. "I don't see a problem," he said. "The ground's probably worth that."

Everyone looked at him.

"Well—that's the truth. You take the last sale out near Johnsville for that pizza parlor and you'd come close to that value—or more."

"That was a smaller piece," George said. "Smaller pieces always bring more per square foot."

"It was—but you'd get synergy with a bigger piece like this. I like owning a piece of it," Stoddard said and returned his eyes to watching the coffee go around in his cup.

"So it would cost us each about $250,000?" RuthAnn said.

Hawk nodded.

She looked at Wev who had his hands crossed in his lap, sitting bent backed in the chair. He nodded, his eyes and lips down at the edges.

George looked around the table. "How are you on this, Hawk?"

Hawk shook his head. "I want to know where you are before I say."

George had filled half a page with doodles, his eyes stuck on the paper in front of him. "I guess I can handle it."

"Ok. We do it then. I want a commitment from each of

you. Five minutes after we close Stoddard is out there taking photos of the land, George is preparing the brochure info, Wev is getting the soils and legal info and RuthAnn is mocking up a brochure and getting a mailing list to send that thing to every builder, developer, investor this side of Lincoln, Nebraska.

"We could develop it ourselves," Stoddard said.

"Sure," Hawk said. "We've made *so* much money developing."

"We've never had a piece free and clear before."

"To pay taxes, assessments on. Haul away trashed cars, batteries and old appliances and pick up fisherman's trash. Yeah—we need that," RuthAnn said.

"What do you think, Wev?" Stoddard said.

"I just want to get this thing closed." He shook his head. "I'm sick of it."

"Do I have your commitments?" Hawk asked. He looked around the table and each person nodded.

"Ok—you each have a part of this closing. Get your signed agreements over to the escrow. Call each of the individual owners and make sure they understand where they are to go today in their locale to sign and close. If you run into any problems let me know pronto."

"Hawk?" George said. "What do we end up with property wise?"

"We get that 640 acres…"

"Rocks and rattlesnakes," Stoddard edged in.

"…inside Slim's ranch, with an easement to it and $3 million dollars worth of Indian land."

George nodded.

"Go to it," Hawk said.

9:00 a.m. Friday, June 12, 1998

"You got any Pepto-Bismol?"

"No," RuthAnn said. "Wev might."

Wev opened his drawer and pulled some out.

Hawk went into the bathroom. He hung his coat on the hook and dashed his face with cool water, took the Pepto-Bismol. In two minutes he threw it and his breakfast up. He knew the fan wouldn't cover the sounds of his physical problems but he didn't care. It wasn't like he had a choice.

Back in his office he dialed Slim's number.

"Morning Slim. Get your cattle ready to move to that high ground in August. We're closing it today. You know where to go?"

"There's only six buildings in town—reckon I can find it. Everyone else signed did they?"

"Yup." Hawk held his breath.

"Ok—me and the Missus will go in there before noon."

"Call me if you have any questions when you get there," Hawk said.

"Don't worry about that. When you coming down this way again?"

"Don't know."

"Call me when you do. I miss your BS."

Hawk chuckled. "I will."

He hung up and started calling the list of other private owners, verbally guiding each to the escrow that was closing the transaction in their area. He finished around 10:30 and felt hungry.

No wonder. Threw my breakfast into the sewer system.

"I'm going for coffee and a cinnamon roll—any guests?"

Stoddard and George stood up and started for the door. Wev was ten steps behind. They took a booth and waited for the rolls to heat.

"Any problems?" Hawk said.

They all shook their heads.

"Everybody knew about it from our letter," Stoddard said.

"Seems like a waste of time," Wev said.

"Backup," Hawk said. "Tell them what you're going to

tell them, tell them, then tell them what you told them. Always works."

Wev was silent. Hawk didn't want to push it. As long as Wev made his calls that was all Hawk expected of him at this moment. He had reached his personal Peter Principal. Another day of this and he might crack wide open. The last two weeks he had been sullen, but the closing check would give a lift to his smile.

They were half way through the cinnamon rolls when Hawk's cell phone rang.

"Hawk," a voice said. "This is Gloria at Inland Escrow. We've called to verify funds on your checks and the bank says the $35,000 won't clear."

Hawk pulled the phone away from his face. "Shit!" he hissed.

"What?" Gloria said.

"Who did you talk to?"

"I don't know—the cashier who answered I guess."

"Talk to Carroll," Hawk said.

"I asked for him but he was out. I see your note here to call him but…"

"I'll take care of it Gloria. Call you back soon. Thanks for notifying me."

Hawk slid the phone in his pocket. "Now where would Carroll go thirty minutes after the bank opened?" Hawk said.

They all looked interested in the answer.

11:15 a.m. Friday, June 12, 1998

Carroll was in the barbershop bent back in the chair with a hot towel over his face.

"Is that Carroll Swenson under there?" Hawk asked.

"Which Carroll Swenson?" the barber asked.

"The one paying for this haircut with my money."

"Not so loud, Hawk. I'm resting," Carroll said.

"You're supposed to do that at night, not when escrow is

calling to verify funds and they get some stupid clerk who tells them the check won't clear."

Carroll whipped off the towel. "Oh my God."

"That's the proper response." Hawk dialed the escrow and handed his cell phone to Carroll.

"What are you doing?" Carroll said.

"Tell Gloria the check is good."

Carroll put his hand on the phone. "Put it away Hawk. I'm not going to talk to her now." He motioned with his eyes and a nod of his head at the barber.

"When?"

"I'll be done here in a few minutes. Meet me at the bank at 11:30."

"No. I'll sit here and walk back to the bank with you," Hawk said.

11:30 a.m. Friday, June 12, 1998

"I didn't want to talk in front of him," Carroll said. "I don't need any other people knowing that I'm verifying money on a no-good check."

"It's not no-good and you know it. It closes and it's good."

"At this moment it is no good. We both know that."

"So what—it isn't illegal."

Carroll shook his head as they walked. "I want to do the bank's business from the bank, not from a barbershop. Is that alright with you?"

"It is if you do your work and don't let some trainee-clerk foul up my escrow."

"Oh, Hawk," Carroll breathed a sigh. "You're a hard guy to love."

"Maybe you can't love me but you sure can do what you said you were going to do when you said you were going to do it!"

Inside they went into Carroll's office and closed the door. Carroll called the escrow and verified the check was good and could be processed at the closing.

"Thank you," Hawk said.

"I said I'd do it and I did. I hope I can come to work for you if the board fires me over this."

"The board isn't going to fire you. Not when you control about $20 million in deposits first of the week."

"That much?"

Hawk nodded. "You insured for that much?"

"Hell no. FDIC only goes to $100,000 on each account. We'll find a way to keep it insured and get it working for you."

"First thing I'm gonna need is a loan to develop that Indian land out on the curve," Hawk said.

Carroll looked up. "You're getting that?"

"Yes. Cruit and company forced it down our throats."

Carroll raised his eyebrows. "That's good ground. Les Schaub was in here last week looking for a new site for his tire store. Might work for him."

Hawk smiled.

There it was—lemons into lemonade. Things like that had happened all his life. Like the guy in England who bought the citrus fruit from a Spanish ship just before it spoiled and made marmalade. Made a fortune when the ship's captain thought he was losing a fortune.

"Well—I'll have to call Schaub on that. Thanks."

"Let's get together Monday and ring in that deposit, shall we?"

"Right after breakfast," Hawk said. "Right after *you* buy breakfast."

12:00 Noon Friday, June 12, 1998

"I'm going to lunch," Stoddard said. "Any company?"

"Not hungry," Hawk said.

"Me neither," Wev said.

Hawk stood up and stretched. "Who's getting the BIA approval for the new sales price on the land?"

They all looked blank.

"Why does BIA have to approve it? Stoddard said. "They agreed to the $2 million deal why wouldn't they go for this?"

"Because they are a government agency and anytime you change the terms and conditions they need to approve it. Why do I have to think of everything around here?" Hawk said.

"Easy, Hawk," Stoddard said. "We're all under a lot of tension. Let's just solve the problem and move on to the closing,"

"So—who's going to do it?"

George spoke up, "I'll do it." He picked up the file and was out the door before anyone spoke again.

The other three looked at each other with expressionless faces. Sweat beaded on Stoddard's forehead. It was close enough to feel the anxiety and after an awkward minute they each turned and went their own way.

The phone rang in Hawk's office. It was the escrow closer.

"Mr. Neilson, the two land parcels your group is getting—what name are you taking them in?"

"Pine Ridge Properties LLC."

"Well—that's what it says here but that name is not registered with the state and our records show no formation of it. Did you complete the registration of the limited liability company with the corporation commissioner?"

"Oh my God—I'll get right back to you. Don't go away."

"I'm leaving for lunch right now. Call me back in about forty-five minutes—ok?"

"Ok."

"Stoddard," Hawk yelled through the open door.

Stoddard ambled in and leaned against the door jam.

"Did we ever finish the set up for the limited liability company we worked on with Thaddeus?"

Stoddard shook his head. "Don't know. Wev was handling that."

"Where is he? We need to take title in that company's name if we want to avoid taxes on that portion of this deal."

Stoddard nodded. "I know but..."

"Did it get to Thaddeus?"

Stoddard looked stunned. "I expect so."

"You or me?" Hawk said.

"You know Thaddeus better," Stoddard said. "You can work him."

"I'll do it."

Thaddeus was not in his office. Hawk left a message on his answering machine and started for the restaurant. He knew not to go to Ella's so he looked in the Elks Club lounge and there enjoying a medium rare tenderloin was the heart of the legal community in Rapid City.

"Hawk—will you join me?" Thaddeus said.

"I don't eat heavy lunches."

"You should. Hold your guts in place until scotch time."

"How long you going to be?"

"Am I supposed to be somewhere?" He stopped his fork and looked at Hawk. "Stop bouncing your leg, you're making me nervous."

"I need that LLC to record today."

Thaddeus took a bite and chewed deliberately. "Can't do it. Has to go through state registration before you can record it."

"We can do it. Hurry up."

Thaddeus set his knife and fork down and ran the napkin over his lips. "Hawk—first it has to be finished, then stamped by the state corporation commission, then recorded."

"Have to hurry. Need to get it done before 3 o'clock. Put the steak in a doggie bag and let's go. Waitress, could we have a doggie bag here, please?"

"Dammit Hawk. Do all the people you work with have to live this screwed up life you live?"

"Just today. By this weekend you'll never remember you had this steak—you'll order another one."

"We'll never get it done," Thaddeus said.

"Quit being so negative and move."

12:37 p.m. Friday, June 12, 1998

Thaddeus and Hawk sat in the office going over the file the legal secretary had brought in.

"Not much left to do," Thaddeus said. "My last notes on it were to wait until I heard from you."

"You're hearing now. What do you need to know?"

"Who's in the company, what units do they own and how much it is capitalized for? That's about it."

Hawk gave him the information and went back to his office while the final corporation papers were being processed. At 1:32 p.m. he picked them up from Thaddeus' office and drove them to the airport. The pilot was waiting.

"Land on that little grass strip near the capital park in Boise. I'll call a taxi and have him waiting to pick you up. Take these straight to the commissioner's office, get them stamped and recorded, then fly that thing back here like it had a tail wind. Here's $500 cash for anything you need to pay for. Get going."

Hawk didn't get out of third gear driving back from the airport. He parked in the alley and jogged in, picked up the phone and dialed the governor's office.

"Governor Prichard's office, Celia speaking."

"Hello, Celia. This is Hawkins Neilson—is the governor in?"

"He's just out for a minute—will you hold, Mr. Neilson?"

"Yes—thank you."

There was a click and a pause.

"No, I don't want to invest in any of your harebrained schemes!"

"Governor Prichard—how nice of you to answer the phone."

"It was sitting here. What's happening on the river?"

"Fish are jumping and the cotton is high..." Hawk sang.

"You been drinking?"

"I need some of your high powered assistance..."

"Yes..."

"Would you call the corporation commissioner and ask him to stamp and record a new company for me pronto. It's being flown in—be there in about twenty minutes. I gotta have it back here before 3 o'clock."

"Seems a little tight on time doesn't..."

"Yes it is. But I recall several times during the last campaign when the TV station wasn't going to air your ad without payment in advance and..."

"You have a good memory, Hawk. If you could just fish as good as you can remember..."

"Will you do it?"

"Sure. What's the name of the company?"

"Pine Ridge Properties LLC," Hawk said.

"You got it." Hawk could hear the pen scratching on paper. "When's the best time to catch one of those big steelhead?"

"Come on down anytime Governor. I hear they're jumping in the boats."

"Your dynamiting them in probably."

"You're thinking of cat fish—not steelhead," Hawk said.

"Guess you're right. I'll get a break here in a couple of weeks and maybe we can wet a line or two, have a drink, talk about the next election."

Hawk could picture the Governor, leaned back in his chair looking at the mounted steelhead on the wall. "You going to run again?"

"Why not? I haven't got anything else to do."

"You could work as a consultant for us."

"Well—if I get whipped I might just do that. What's it pay?"

"Our standard wage for a consultant of your caliber is $1.85 an hour plus board and room."

"You tell my wife that, I'll have to run again."

Hawk chuckled. "Thanks, Governor."

"Glad to help, Hawk."

Chapter 15

2:34 p.m. Friday, June 12, 1998

George Arbuckle walked into the office and laid the manila folder titled BIA on Hawk's desk. He wasn't exactly smiling but he had a sense of satisfaction resting on his face.

"Signed?" Hawk said.

"Signed, sealed, and delivered."

Hawk reached for it. "Good man, George. The big muckity-muck sign it himself?"

George nodded. "He whistled some at the price and allowed as how he should have bought that land."

"Yeah—on his salary. It's been there long enough to qualify as a burial grounds."

RuthAnn stuck her head in the door, "The pilot called in—he's ten minutes from landing."

"You want me to go get it?" George said.

"Naw—I'll get it. I need to do something to keep from going nuts."

Hawk pulled out his file. Did I forget anything?

In the other time zones ranchers and farmers were already signing and the escrows had scheduled their recordings to be completed before the end of the day. When the world woke up on Monday morning, some two million acres will have changed hands, over $400 million worth of property and each of the four people in his office would walk into their bank and deposit a check for about $3 million. That would be a day.

He grabbed his key ring, containing keys to everything he had access to and headed for the car. There was time to meet the airplane and make the escrow at 3:00 p.m. so he drove within the speed limit. He mentally clicked off each item that he had on his to-do sheet—they were all done.

For some reason, how much he was going to award Sue Diggs for her work on the deal—something he had never placed a figure on—worked its way into his thinking. Even as he tried to blink it away the visual image of her standing in the doorway asking how much her share was, kept plodding back.

Everyone thinks when a guy has $13 million he can give away $4 million and still be wealthy. Should I give her a portion based on a percentage, or what she needs, or just pick a figure and leave it at that? What if she's unhappy with it? How about very unhappy? How about pissed?

A hundred thousand would be several years' income for her—that should do it. Course—we spent four years on this sucker—maybe four years average income. Make that two hundred thousand. She should be tickled pink with that. I would be. Really? No—but then I've borne the brunt of this thing from beginning to end. Conceived it, started it, and now will see it born. On the other hand, Sue was there every step of the way. She was there when I was down, sick, depressed. And when I was up—charged up to the max—couldn't sleep. Every time I looked, every time I needed her she was there. She cooked, she cleaned, she massaged, she worked intransigent ranchers and agency heads. Really—she had no piece of this, no outright recognition that her efforts would help in the culmination but she did what I asked without question. Just took off and did it—and did it well. Of the things she did, none of them came back to bite us. I'll have to come up with something for her.

What's next? I guess getting rid of the land we picked up from BLM and the Indian piece, or develop it. If Les Schwab doesn't buy, he would make a great anchor tenant for other businesses.

Think of the breathing room—just think of it. Pay everything and—and what? Retire?

He drove under the airport entry gate. The pilot had walked halfway between the parked airplane and the flight office when Hawk pulled along side and rolled down the window.

"Have any problems?" Hawk said.

The pilot handed the papers over. "Just one. That old grass strip isn't being used anymore. Had to land at the flight service and taxi in. Here's what's left of your $500." He gave him a wad of money but held out ten dollars. "Late lunch," he said.

"Fair enough. I really appreciate it. Bill my office for your time."

The pilot smiled. "What about the speed—and the risk?"

"Screw that," Hawk said. "That's why you fly."

3:00 p.m. Friday, June 12, 1998

The receptionist at Inland Escrow paged Sandy Jackson to notify her that Mr. Hawkins Neilson was there to see her.

Hawk was stirring a cup of hot chocolate when Sandy came in, a broad smile on her face.

"You actually think we're going to close this today?" she said.

"Sandy—you'd better have a cemetery lot picked out if we don't."

She threw her head back. "Got a nice one with a view of the river under some trees where the snow doesn't get on it."

"I'm hoping you won't need it for awhile yet," Hawk said.

"Me too. The others are here—let's go into the conference room."

Sandy led the way through the hallway into the large conference room, her perfume lending a feminine touch to the event. Seated in the high-backed leather chairs and standing around the mahogany table were his team members.

George Arbuckle as usual with his legal pad, two pens, and a calculator in front of him nursed a cup of coffee. Stoddard Greening stood behind his chair doing a thoughtful job of tamping tobacco in a pipe he wouldn't smoke until he was outside the building. In front of him on the table was a large file. Wev and RuthAnn were at the far end closest to where Sandy took her seat. RuthAnn had her calculator and a pad, pencil, and eraser to proof the figures when they were presented. Two file boxes that held individual parcels and owner's information were in front of Wev on the table.

"I think we're ready," Sandy said. She handed out copies of the charts she had prepared of who gave up what and who got what and the full name of the grantor and grantee and asked for the various documents that both George and Stoddard had brought with them.

When that was done Hawk provided her with the new company registration papers, the employee identification number, and a list of the investors in the LLC.

"Everything looks ok," she said. "I need to call the individual escrow offices now in each state and verify that they've gotten their documents signed and then we can all record before

5 o'clock in our individual time zones. Do you want to stay here or shall I call one of you and let you know?"

They looked at one another. Four years of blood, sweat and tears, unrelenting strife, thousands of decisions, moments of sheer panic—and now how to answer this one question? Could they just sit there, doing nothing, waiting for the phone to ring, while escrows were closing across the western United States? Did they have other urgent things to do? Would it be important if they ever did anything again? None of them had ever done anything like this and would not likely do so again. The conclusion had them breathing slowly, their respiration rate just a notch above sleep and it was late in the afternoon, a Friday, and warm. No one spoke. Hawk looked at each in turn.

"Call me," he said. "We're not doing anything useful here." He stood up, pushed the chair back with his legs and walked out the door.

4:30 p.m. Friday, June 12, 1998

Back in his office, he had just sat down and was leaning back in his chair when the phone rang.

"Hello, Hawk," Slim said his phone voice scratchy around the edges. "We closed here and the escrow gal just called me. Told me she recorded and everything went well. I want to mail you a bottle of scotch—what's your favorite?"

"You can't mail whiskey—it's against the law," Hawk said.

"Watch me."

Hawk chuckled. "Well it's Lagavulin. It's a fine single malt from the Isle of Islay, lots of smoke and peat odors, but you won't find it in your hamlet."

"It may surprise you to know that we can get stuff from all over the world. And listen—that invite still stands. When you get down this way let's sit on the porch, kick off our boots and hoist a few. I'm not getting any younger—neither are you. We're going to wake up one of these days and realize we didn't spend enough time with people we like, and dammit—you're a fine man."

"Thank you, Slim. I appreciate that—I truly do."

"The Missus is telling me we gotta get back to the ranch. She gets nervous about me driving after dark. Well—just wanted to say thank you for the time and energy and persistence you put into this…"

"…And money," Hawk stuck in.

"…and money, and that I won't shoot at you when you start building that road into the 640 sitting in the middle of my North pasture."

"Thanks for calling, Slim. I'll stop when I get down that way. Tell your wife thanks too."

Hawk hung up the phone and saw Cruit waving an envelope at him through the window. He motioned him in.

"What brings you into my humble office?" Hawk said.

"Gratitude."

"Really?" Hawk raised his eyebrows. "Should I be leery?"

"No more so than we were when you put us on reservations."

"Oh—then I'm leery."

"Good idea." Cruit opened the envelope and put a letter on Hawk's desk.

Hawk picked it up and started reading. He glanced at the date. "This is dated three days ago."

"I know," Cruit said.

Hawk looked at him skeptically. "You kept it quiet?"

Cruit shook his head. "I told the council."

"And they agreed?"

Cruit nodded.

"And this second letter—an assignment?"

Cruit nodded again. "Yes. Signed by all of the council."

"That makes it pretty binding then doesn't it?" Hawk said.

"You probably wouldn't believe a law clerk anyway, but I'd say it is."

Hawk nodded his head, a slow steady pressure building behind the top of his eyes, the moisture filling his eyelids. He took one hand off the paper, pulled out a handkerchief and wiped his nose.

He wet his lips with his tongue and looked at Cruit.

"We got everything we wanted," Cruit said. "Now it's your turn." He smiled, stood up, walked out of the office, across the room and out the brand new door onto the street.

Stoddard watched Cruit leave then stuck his head in Hawk's office. "What'd he want?"

Hawk shook his head but couldn't speak. His eyes misted. He handed him the letter, shoved his hands in his pockets and looked out the window while Stoddard read.

When he finished reading he stared at the document for a full minute, then let his hands slip down to his side. He followed Hawk's gaze out the window. In a soft voice he said, "Doesn't make sense."

Hawk swallowed and blinked. "Sure it does. Makes perfect sense."

George and Wev filed in. They looked at Stoddard standing mute, the paper unoffered to them clutched in his hand. George lifted the document from Stoddard's hand and read the letter.

"Is it true?" he asked.

"Appears so," Hawk said.

Wev jumped up and flung his arms over his head. "Hot digidy damn,"

A broad smile creased Hawk's face. "My sentiments exactly,"

George Arbuckle looked up from the letter. "Now why would they do something like that?"

Hawk snorted. "They've never made any money developing. They don't have the talent or the capital to do it themselves, but more importantly, it doesn't fit their life style or their self-image. They're going to do what they know and love best—being Indians with land, horses, buffalo, fish in clear running rivers. Some will go to college, get degrees, come back and help out and they'll have a nation to run. The Nez Perce Nation—got a good ring to it, doesn't it?"

"I guess," George said. He laid the document carefully on top of the other and straightened it on the desk.

RuthAnn stood in the door. "I heard it but I don't understand it," she said.

"Les Schwab offered to lease the Indian land long term. They talked it over, decided they would rather have the money now. We had it so they asked for it; then assigned the proposed lease agreement to us."

"Who's us?"

"Pine Ridge Properties LLC," Hawk said

"So we won't be holding that property for another twelve years like they did?"

"Not if we execute this lease agreement."

She turned on her heel and walked back to her desk. She sat down with her hands in her lap and stared out the window, emotions drained. She couldn't concentrate, or smile or frown. She blinked several times and continued staring out the window.

Hawk stepped to his office door. "RuthAnn—would you please draw the checks."

She shook her head; came out of her trance. "What for?" she said. "It's after 5 o'clock now, they can't cash them."

Hawk smiled. "I doubt anybody's going to be cashing a $3 million check today, but the bank's open until 6. They might want to deposit them."

"Oh—ok."

Hawk picked up the phone and dialed Royal's number.

"This is Royal."

"Royal—Hawk here. You can put your checkbook away, didn't need it. But thank you for being ready to do it."

"Glad you got it done." He sounded genuinely happy.

"Course—I'm always sorry to miss out on points and interest."

"I can understand that. However, we got you a good price for that mountain top," Hawk said.

"That was a mountain meadow—long summer grass— fair value," Royal said.

Hawk could hear a drawer open, then close.

Royal said, "On a non-business note what are you going to do this weekend?"

"Think I'll sit on the bank of the river, throw in a line, read a few pages in Gale Ontko's new book, **Thunder Over the Ochoco**, and sip some good scotch whiskey."

"Sounds absolutely delightful. I should try that some-time."

"You really should. Does wonders for a person."

"Maybe when I'm your age…."

"Come on, Royal, we're not that far apart."

"Soon. I'll give that a whirl very soon."

"Goodbye, Royal."

5:37 p.m. Friday, June 12, 1998

"Please put each check in a separate envelope with the person's name on it," Hawk said.

RuthAnn handed him the four unsealed envelopes. He took them back to his office, signed each check, stuffed them in the envelope and sealed them. He stood up, walked to the door and called them in one at a time, handed them their envelope and asked them to wait. They stood in a semi-circle in front of his desk, Wev and RuthAnn each holding one end of their enve-lope.

"There's a little over $3 million to each of you. I'm not wanting to tell you what to do with it, but save a little for a rainy day. We've put aside a million to deal with the Indian land, but as you know, Les Schwab is asking to lease it so we should get that back. We'll need a little to build the road through Slim's ranch and sell that piece, but we've got enough for that."

Hawk stood up, put a long straight arm on the desk and cleared his throat. "There've been times when I've been hard to live with—I know that. You've all been fair and done good work. This is my..." He cleared his throat and swallowed. "... my last..." He put his tongue between his teeth, bit down, shook his head. "I won't be in Monday. I won't be back— ever."

6:50 p.m. Friday, June 12, 1998

"Hawk—stop that."

"Come on, you know you like it."

"I've got a sunburn—it hurts."

"Where'd you get a sunburn?"

"I stood in the hay field for two hours yesterday waiting for Charlie Nelson to finish with a load so I could talk to him," Sue Diggs said.

"Did he go for it?"

"He wants to think it over—he'd love to have some land on that slope. Doesn't know if he wants to fight the rocks and rattlesnakes for it though."

"That big D8 of his would eat both of those up in a week," Hawk said.

"That's what I told him."

"He make a pass at you?"

"Just a little one. It was hot out there."

"Here—drink some of this. Cool you off.'

She took a sip of the weak vodka-tonic. "You made it just right—not too strong."

Hawk smiled. "I have learned something about what you like. Oh—I forgot. There's a letter for you. I put it on the mantle," Hawk said.

"Who's it from?"

Hawk shook his head and sipped the Lagavulin.

Sue set her drink down and got the envelope. She opened it and froze. Tears came to her eyes then tumbled down her cheeks and soaked into her blouse. She held the envelope away from her and cried.

Gently he lifted the envelope from her hand and set it back on the mantle. He wrapped his arms around her while she sobbed.

"Oh, Hawk, Hawk, Hawk…"

He patted her back, sunburn be damned.

"I never dreamed…" she started.

"Yeah you did. It was the sort of thing we both dreamed about wasn't it?"

She nodded, quivered, the tears streaking her makeup. "A million dollars…I've never seen that much money…is it real?"

He handed her his handkerchief.

She giggled between sobs. "Looks like it's been used."

"Matter of fact it was," he said. "Had a moment myself today."

"When?"

"Cruit brought in the lease that was signed three days ago."

Sue pulled her head back, her forehead and eyes formed a question. "That brought you to tears?"

"I guess it did. Seemed so up and up. Nothing back-stabbing or lawyer-ish about it. Just a gesture that after all of this…the fairness of it…the kindness…"

"Oh, Hawk—you're a sentimental baby aren't you? You are."

"And you?"

Sue looked at the check, smiled and clutched it to her chest.

Hawk fished in his pocket and brought out a small velvet green envelope. He looked at it between his fingers; his lips pursed, then held it up for her to see. When she was looking directly at it he extended his arm toward her and smiled.

"You're full of surprises aren't you?" she said as she accepted the cracker sized velvet package. Her finger tips told her what it was but they didn't describe the beauty of it.

She took the ring from the envelope and slid it on her finger. "Hawk—it's beautiful. So beautiful…"

"You put it on the wrong finger." He pulled it off and put it on her left hand ring finger.

Sue brought her eyes up to his. "Does this mean…."

Hawk nodded. "If you want it to."

She threw her arms around him. "Oh yes, yes, yes, yes, yes yes…"

He held her pressed against him. His nose inhaled the fresh scent of her hair, her sobs retreating, her tears dripping onto his shirt.

She tilted her head back and looked him in the eye. "Does this make me the most expensive mistress in Jefferson County?

"I've been thinking about that," Hawk started. "Actually…it was this transaction. I gave birth to it, raised it…was wedded to it for four years without a marriage license. Mortgaged my house, spent everything I had on it. Cared for it, nursed it, gave it CPR," he shook his head, "and it ate my lunch many times."

Sue traced a line with her finger down his cheek. "I'm jealous."

Hawk smiled, reached for his glass. "Why don't you refresh my scotch and I'll sit here and figure out how I can make it up to you."

Readers comments on Misko's prior novel
FOR WHAT HE COULD BECOME

"Great book! Cathy got hold of it first and almost could not put it down until she finished it. She NEVER reads a book. Then my turn. I didn't like it, I loved it. The story was so true to life and what I have seen so many times throughout Alaska. The race part was so perfect that I got cold, was elated, depressed, all the emotions one gets while actually running. It took me out on the trail again, especially the early years. Congratulations."

Dick Mackey, Winner of the 1978 Iditarod
Author: ONE SECOND TO GLORY

"I was not expecting a full-blown action and emotion packed, transporting reading experience. I could not put it down, and once the race started, did not. When I had finished, I reread it cover to cover. In forty years of fairly steady and broad-based book devouring, I have seldom done that! You are in good company; Kipling, Faulkner, and Scott."

Skip Lynar

"The author quickly and expertly draws the reader into the life of a promising native Alaskan youth. A bond is formed, and you will find yourself emotionally involved as the character struggles to adjust to life outside the village from world war to a climactic sled dog race. It's a roller coaster of a life, but worth the ride. Not a boring moment."

J. Bell, Esquire

"I finished this action-filled novel at 4:00 a.m. and my heart was still pounding with excitement. Jim Misko develops his characters so well that they become alive with their illustrative experiences. He builds the main character from a listless youth that continues to break out of the expected mold into a young man who, in spite of tragic experiences achieves personal victory through his persistent determination, desire, and dedication. My only warning to the reader is that once the Iditarod Race starts, you will not be able to put the book down. "For What He Could Become" is similar to the book and recent hit movie "Cold Mountain," only it has so much more depth in the character and excitement in the story."

G. Dennis Vaughan Rear Admiral, United States Navy (Retired)

"Great book. Brilliantly narrated; gut wrenching story."

George Wingard

Author: WOLVES IN SHEEP'S CLOTHING

"For What He Could Become" became a favorite of the year on my current list of books.

Jeanne Tallman

"I like how you are able to so vividly describe in detail –you feel like you are there and can visualize the surroundings, the characters, etc. The story line is one that is hard to put the book down once you begin because you want to know what will happen next. It is very "real." It sounds/feels like you had visited with an individual and wrote about what really happened to him."

Corinne Hawley, Librarian

"Jim Misko has lived in Alaska for over three decades and his writing reflects the deep research he has done in capturing the spirit of our 49th State. Not since Robert Service and Jack London has an author expressed the realities of life in the land...This novel is a page turner that captivates and holds the reader's interest until the very last page. Live the adventure in this very exciting book."

Mary Barrer, Book Reviewer for Miami Westchester World

Just finished your novel today, could not put it down. The story of Bill Williams and his battle for redemption, moved me. From the prospective of an Alaskan, the novel is a reflection of the places and people we live with. Many people come to the last frontier for a chance for adventure and/or redemption. This novel encompasses both.

Keith Henson

Readers Comments:
THE MOST EXPENSIVE MISTRESS IN JEFFERSON COUNTY

"Most entertaining, uplifting book I've read all year. Makes me wish he would write a novel a month. Having spent a good deal of my life in real estate, I can feel for the protagonist as he gets caught up in trying to close that large of a transaction, knowing he has every chip he owns in the deal. What a close one."

Don Jack

"I tried, but I couldn't put it down. I ate lunch reading it, then scotch at 5:00, then dinner, alone at the dining room table with the lights full on, and finished it in bed. What a ride. Gimmie another one."

Darry Gemmell

"Realistic, relentless, exciting. I found myself wondering if I knew the characters, they seemed too true to life - like I had met them somewhere in my career."

Leann Curro

"This is Great Stuff! I could not put this down in spite of having a business associate in town for two days."

Mary Ann Shaughnessy Krum

"Misko sets the tension in motion early, immediately increases it to fever pitch, then sustains it as one escalating crescendo. A variety of three dimensional and sympathetic characters drive the plot to a realistic and entirely satisfactory conclusion."

Leonard Bird, author of River Of Lost Souls and Folding Paper Cranes, an Atomic Memoir

"The characters were so real I could see, smell and feel each one and see inside their heads. Their emotions were mine. The humor had me laughing out loud while tears of tension and frustration welled in my eyes. The dialogue was faultless and kept the pages crackling. You have captured the essence of Native Americans with sensitivity and understanding. And you have given heart to a big business deal. Thanks for a great read."

Jeanne Tallman

To my readers.

Thank you for buying my books. The publishing business is changing faster than most traditional publishers can change and many are consolidating, going on-line, and reinterpreting how they connect with the readers who buy books.

I have found that along with Barnes & Noble, Borders, Amazon, and Google Books, there are hundreds of other ways to reach book readers. One is through book clubs. Several book clubs have purchased by first novel and are awaiting this book, THE MOST EXPENSIVE MISTRESS IN JEFFERSON COUNTY. I keep track of all the buyers I can so that I can send them notice of my succeeding books.

If you want to ask me any questions, have me speak to your book club or any other group who buys books, or find out how to start an Authors Guild or host a Writers Workshop, I'm here for you. E-mail me to find out how we can do that.

Therefore—if you would like to be in my "readers club" and get a notice of when I will be in your area for a book signing, put out a new book, endure some new challenge, I'll be happy to do it. Just fill in below, please.

You can always reach me through my web site: www.JimMisko.com

Your Name:

Your E-mail:

Repeat E-mail

Address (if you wish)

Phone (if you wish)

You are currently subscribed to Jim Misko reader club as _____

____
To unsubscribe send an email to jim@jimmisko.com and request removal.

All names and email addresses are kept confidential. They are not shared with anyone.

Contact:

9138 Arlon Street
Suite A3-881
Anchorage, AK 99507
jim@jimmisko.com

Jim Misko grew up in Ord, Nebraska, moved to Oregon, and then to Alaska. He has worked as a schoolteacher, roughneck, mink rancher, truck driver, logger, and real estate broker. This is his second novel. Jim and his wife, Patti, live in Anchorage, Alaska in the summer and La Quinta, California in the winter.

His third novel, THE CUT OF PRIDE, will be published in 2008.